Mary: To Protect Her Heart

Mary: To Protect Her Heart

Mansfield Park Continuation, Episode 3

LEENIE BROWN

LEENIE B BOOKS
HALIFAX

Contents

Dear Reader,

At the end of *Mansfield Park*, Jane Austen wrote:

> *Let other pens dwell on guilt and misery. I quit such
> odious subjects as soon as I can, impatient to restore
> everybody not greatly in fault themselves to tolera-
> ble comfort and to have done with all the rest.*

It is my goal in writing the books found in the *Other Pens
Collection* to take up my pen and continue the stories of
various Austen characters who were at fault in some way
in Miss Austen's novels. In these stories of redemption
and reformation, I do not look to dwell on the characters'
guilt and misery so much as help them find a way to over-
come their failures and find their own happiness.

These stories are not retellings or even variations. They
are continuations, which begin with at least one Austen
character and spread outward as the change from in that
one individual's life influences the lives of others in his or
her circle of friends and family.

The book you hold in your hand is one of my *Mansfield*

Park Continuation Episodes, which began after the close of *Manfield Park* with Henry Crawford deciding to prove himself worthy of a good woman. While each episode contains a complete happily ever after for its hero and heroine, it is assumed that the reader knows about the events in the preceding books. Therefore, while reading in any order may be done, for maximum enjoyment, reading all of the books in order is recommended.

Chapter 1

Mary Crawford watched her brother's friend, Charles Edwards, walk away from her. Anger and hurt warred within her. If she could just make the anger stronger than the pain of yet another rejection, she would be able to keep her chin held high and the tears where they should be – locked away. Tears were a sign of weakness, something upon which a gentleman could ply his game. She was not the sort of lady who would be a pawn in some gentleman's game.

"That was rather harsh. Not undeserved, I would venture, but harsh," someone said behind her.

"Indeed, it was!" Mr. Tenley, with whom she was supposed to dance, agreed forcefully.

Mary steeled her spine and turned toward the gentleman behind her. "Mr. Bertram."

Tom Bertram gave her a small bow. "Miss Crawford." He greeted. "I am well, and so is most of my family." He offered without her inquiring. "Fanny and Edmund will have a child before the summer is through. Julia and Yates already have a daughter, and, in case you have not heard, it is unlikely that Maria will ever have the joy of being a mother."

"Now, just a moment," Mr. Tenley interjected. "I do not like the tone you are using with Miss Crawford."

Tom made a small, bitter laughing sound. "I do not like the abominable way in which Miss Crawford and her brother used my family. But, I will agree that this is not the best place for such a discussion." He turned from the man sputtering beside Mary to her. "I cannot dance every set." He lifted his cane. "And I prefer to save those sets for ladies who might fill the role of Lady Bertram when I come into my inheritance. However, if you have a set free, there is a well-lit path in the garden upon which we might stroll."

Mary regarded him warily. "You wish to walk with me?"

He nodded.

"Why?" She knew how his family's reputation had been damaged when her brother, due to her meddling, had run off with Tom's sister, who was, at that time, married. The marriage had not survived the affair, and now Maria Bertram was a disgraced and divorced woman. There was no reason in Mary's mind for Mr. Bertram to be kind to her.

"I wish to know the whole of the ugliness in which my sister was involved. I have had time to contemplate life in a serious fashion, and I have decided that I will not bear a grudge against you or your brother. However, I must speak to both of you on the matter, so that it can be settled in my mind." Tom looked across the ballroom to where Henry Crawford stood with a pretty young lady on his arm amidst a group of people. "And since your brother looks as if he is in no mood to be disturbed, I thought I would begin with you, and perhaps that will be enough."

"I – " Mary began to refuse, but then, reconsidering, looked at Mr. Tenley. "Mr. Tenley, would you mind dreadfully if I were to switch this set for the next?" She had very little desire to dance at all with Mr. Tenley, but he had asked.

"I was looking forward to this set," Mr. Tenley replied.

Mary beseeched him with her eyes and pulled her bottom lip between her teeth as she sighed.

"However," Mr. Tenley continued, "if you promise to not leave me standing for the next set."

"Would I do that?" Mary used her most charming voice. Mr. Tenley was one of those gentlemen who was easily led by such things.

"No, I suppose you would not," he replied.

"Then, may I accompany Mr. Bertram to the garden?"

Mr. Tenley nodded.

"You are such an understanding gentleman," Mary praised him. "Some girl is going to be very happy to have you ask for her hand. In fact, if I may make a suggestion, there is a pretty blonde standing by the pillar to our left who has been watching you for some time. I think she would be quite pleased if you were to ask her for a dance. I have not seen anyone approach her yet, but they soon will. She is far too pretty to be a wallflower."

"Is there indeed?" Mr. Tenley turned to look behind them and to the left. "Oh, she is very pretty. Not that I would think you would lead me astray on such things. You are a good judge of beauty."

"Thank you." Mary removed her hand from his arm. "I am certain Mr. Bertram is as grateful as I am that you were so willing to oblige me in this." She looked at Tom, who nodded.

"Most appreciative," he muttered.

"Hurry. You do not wish to lose your chance," Mary encouraged, and Mr. Tenley did as instructed and hurried away. But then, most men did what Mary told them, unless, of course, they were a Bertram or her brother – basically anyone who had come under the influence of some proper chit. It should be she who was increasing with Edmund Bertram's child, not Fanny Price! She could have loved Edmund. She was almost convinced she did love him, even now that he was no longer under her influence.

Tom Bertram extended his arm to her. "This should set the tongues to wagging," he quipped.

She had always liked Tom's ability to not care one wit about what the gossips said. However, he had never paid her any marked attention, and she had seen him dally with ladies and leave them. She would not pursue such a man — no matter how handsome he was or what his inheritance. When she finally decided it was time to marry, she would do as her sister had done and find a fine old fellow who would be far too ancient to care about debutantes and mistresses. He would be happy to have a beauty such as she for his wife, and therefore, she would never have to fear being pushed aside or subjugated to his whims. She had seen enough of that with the admiral. Whomever she married would not be like the admiral. Not at all.

"Has your brother found a lady to accept him?"

Mary nodded. "Miss Linton."

Tom whistled. "Quite a proper young lady, is she not?"

Again, Mary nodded.

"And Edwards seems smitten with Miss Barrett."

"He does."

Tom motioned for her to proceed through the door before him. "I'd not have thought to see him smitten, let alone smitten with one so proper as Miss Barrett."

"Nor would have I," Mary replied.

"I hope to find such a lady myself," Tom confessed. "One who will not make me regret giving up my freedom." He shrugged when she looked at him in surprise. "I have a legacy to secure unless I leave the title and estate to one of Edmund's brood."

"You are giving up your life of pleasure?" What was

becoming of all the fun-loving gentlemen? Why did they all seem to long for some dull lady when they could have their pick of just about anyone?

"I am," he replied. "I nearly died. You do remember that, do you not?"

Oh, she remembered it. She had even imagined it occurring, and Edmund becoming a baronet rather than just a clergyman.

"Such an experience does not leave one unaltered."

"That seems natural," she replied.

"Tenley is wrong for you."

Mary stumbled at such a startling comment.

"He is too easily led. You would grow bored."

"Boring is not bad," Mary said. "Boring is stable."

"Boring is dull. There is a difference between boring and constant. You want constant, not boring."

"I do?"

He nodded. "I have had time to think on many things."

"You thought about me?"

Again, he nodded. "How could I not? I wished to do you harm for some time, but then, I found I could accept what had happened and for my own good, I knew I needed to forgive. Not forget. Not welcome back with open arms. But forgive." He stopped walking. "I do not hold what you and your brother have done to my family against either of you, but I do need to know why. Why would you toy with my family as you did? Why would you conspire to hurt them?"

Mary's mouth dropped open. She had never considered her actions in such a light. For with Tom's questions she saw herself not as the beautiful, vivacious woman she knew herself to be, but as the surly, depraved admiral against whom she had been fighting for so long.

"I... I... I am not certain," she stammered. "I suppose I never thought it would do any harm to have a bit of fun." The words tasted bitter in her mouth as she said them. What a sorry excuse for causing so much pain! A bit of fun! That was what the admiral had always said to his wife. 'I do not know why you are so put out over my having a bit of fun.' She shuttered. How had she become what she loathed?

"I find I might need to sit down." She clutched Tom's arm more tightly as the bushes and lanterns in the garden began to swirl before her. Thankfully, there was a bench nearby. "I do not know what overcame me," she lied as she took a seat. "Perhaps it was the heat of the room giving way to the coolness of the night air so quickly which caused it."

Tom shrugged. "I doubt it." He took a seat next to her, looping his cane over his arm. "I hope to one day be rid of this thing," he said, indicating the cane. "However, I am reliant on it for now." He shifted to look at her. "You never considered the consequences of your game?"

Mary shook her head.

"You would not have liked being a parson's wife," he continued. "That is the one good thing that came from all of this. Your life has not yet been set."

"I would not call it good," she admitted. She would have liked nothing better than to be settled into marriage by now.

"Oh, come now," Tom replied. "You loved the idea of Edmund, but you did not love Edmund. He was easily led – quite naïve and far too good to be anything but. However, I can assure you he is not the sort to be moulded into anything. He might appear to be such, but I have had enough experience in attempting to sway him, and succeeding for a time, only to be disappointed when his sense of duty and morality returned. He can only be fun for so long." Tom chuckled. "I should have listened to his advice years ago, but I did not. I was too bent on pleasure to be hampered with things such as conscience and propriety. But as far as you are concerned, I know beyond a shadow of a doubt he is not the sort of gentleman who would have squired you to parties and shown you off as you deserve. He is quite content to stay in the country and never travel to town."

"I like the country," Mary countered. Before arriving at Mansfield Park, she had begged her brother to set her up at his estate, had she not?

"For a time."

"No, I think I should enjoy remaining in the country." There were far fewer mistresses in the country.

"You would be bored in half a year's time."

"I might have children."

"I still think you would grow bored. You are not the sort of lady one trundles off to the country and hides away. You are far too vivacious for such a thing. But I digress. I am not here to advise you on whom you should marry. I am here to discuss the scandal you helped create."

She had hoped they had left that topic behind. She did not want to discuss it. In fact, she did not even wish to think about it. She had not wanted to think about it before Henry returned to town, and then, she definitely had not wanted to think about it when her brother began citing it as a reason for them to be separated. And she knew quite firmly that she did not want to think about it, now, as Tom had presented it. Any reminder of the admiral was one too many, and any comparison between her and him was reprehensible to even contemplate contemplating. She would rather put the whole sorry business out of her head with a dance or a game of cards or one glass of punch too many.

"There is nothing to discuss. I sought a bit of fun, and it spiralled into something I had never expected. I cannot speak for Henry, of course, but I do not think anything that he did was done maliciously. He was devastated by the loss of Fanny, so I know he did not consider that outcome before he began." She sighed.

Henry had taken the consequences of his actions to heart in a way that Mary was unable to do. While she grieved for her brother's sorrow and her loss of Edmund, she found it difficult to feel remorse for Maria's foolish behaviour, and it was absolutely impossible to even imagine a twinge of regret for Mr. Rushworth. If anything, the whole affair had reinforced what Mary already knew. Ladies – especially foolish ones like Maria Bertram – were the plaything of gentlemen to be used and discarded as needed. Had Maria exhibited some restraint and kept her affair quiet, Mary was still confident it could have been overlooked. Mr. Rushworth was not brilliant. He could easily be fooled. However, his mother was no fool, and therein lay the problem. Maria had not been able to keep the scandal from reaching the ears of Mr. Rushworth's mother, who had a good grasp on both her son and his purse strings.

Tom waved his cane at the door to the ballroom. "This is all a charade. Ladies pretending to be demur. Guardians putting on a good show that love and respect are important when in reality it is money and titles that they truly seek for their charges. And then there are those who are playing for the thrill of the dare – taking what they can get from where they can get it and hoping not to be snared in the process." He shook his head. "I used to find it all exhilarating, but now, I find it rather disgusting." He turned to look at her.

"I did not consider that my actions might result in my death. I was having just a bit of fun, so I can understand and even accept your explanation." His lips curled into a startled grin. "I think it makes it easier for me to forgive you and your brother knowing that you were not purposefully scheming to cause harm. It would not make it easier for Edmund or my father, but for me, having been every bit as you were, it is understandable." He pushed to his feet. "I wasted a large amount of my inheritance and that of my brother without a care for the results until my dissipated ways nearly led to my ultimate demise." He extended a hand to her. "Shall we return? I should hate for you to miss out on a dance with Mr. Tenley."

Mary smiled as she slipped her hand into his. "I would not be sorry to miss it," she admitted.

"So, I am right." There was a note of delight in his tone. "Tenley is boring."

Mary nodded. "And proper."

"Ah, but proper and boring do not need to be the same thing."

"They do not?" In her experience, they had always seemed inseparable. Was that not why she had attempted to sway Edmund away from being a parson? She pulled in a quick breath. Tom was right. Edmund would have been all wrong for her. He would have been loyal, and she would have never had to worry about him taking a mistress. However, she would have likely grown quite bored.

"I intend to be a very interesting proper gent this season."

"You think it is possible?"

"It seems Henry and Edwards are making valiant attempts at it. So, it must be doable."

Mary could not refute that. Her brother and his friend did seem to be quite happy being proper – or nearly proper — and she would not think of either of them as boring.

"You should try it," Tom continued.

"I am all that is proper already," Mary retorted.

Tom laughed. "You are perhaps chaste, but you are not proper. You delight far too much in scandal for me to believe it. And, I would think you would be the sort of lady who would hold her wedding vows tightly only until she had borne the requisite number of children."

Mary stopped walking before they got to the steps which led into the ballroom. "I will not be a mistress to any man whether I am married or not."

"Are you certain?" Tom's tone was slightly mocking, causing Mary to bristle.

"I am positive. I will not be like either the admiral or his wife," she snapped. How could he even suggest such a thing?

"Yet you surround yourself with friends who are, and you encouraged your brother to be such a person." He leveled a hard stare on her. "Prove you are not."

She blinked. How did one prove such a thing other than by getting married and never straying from her husband?

"Proceed through the remainder of the season in a fashion that is opposed to how you have to this point. Find some way to show that you care about something other than yourself. Pick a proper fellow and see if you would suit. I shall be doing the same sort of thing. I am not returning to my old habits and haunts."

"Is this some sort of punishment for having encouraged Henry to attend that dinner party where I knew Maria would be?"

Tom shrugged. "Perhaps it is, but there is nothing compelling you to take my suggestion. So, it would make an ineffective punishment, do you not think?"

Indeed, it would when she considered it as such.

He shrugged again. "Think about it. The alternative could lead to dire consequences." He lifted his cane. "I know of what I speak."

She tipped her head and studied his features. He did not seem to be taunting her. He looked absolutely serious, which, in all the time she had known Tom Bertram, was not an expression he wore very often. "I will give it some thought, but I cannot promise you anything," she finally said. "These things are not so simple for ladies."

"That is all I ask," Tom replied as he led her into the ballroom. "Ah, there is Mr. Tenley." He drew her along the left-hand side of the ballroom to the gentleman. Then, with a bow, he took his leave, but not without first saying, "I look forward to your response."

Mr. Tenley's brows rose halfway to his hairline.

"He wished for some advice," Mary hedged. Then, she smiled brightly. "We do not want to miss our dance, now do we?"

"No, no. Of course, not."

Mr. Tenley was far too easily led. But at present, Mary was happy for it, for it would give her time to sort out some of the troubling thoughts with which Tom Bertram had left her.

Chapter 2

Gabriel Durward glanced up from the paper in front of him and gave a nod of welcome to his friend, Tom Bertram, but continued his conversation with the gentleman seated at the table with him.

"She's American then?"

"She is," the man replied. "A beauty, too."

Gabe studied the manifest in front of him. "You say she was taken clean?"

His companion nodded. "She'll pass the prize court."

If the document he was looking at was correct, the contents of this ship could net him a healthy profit.

"She's worth refitting," his companion suggested.

Another ship? Gabe rubbed his chin. Was he ready to take on another? "I will take a look at her tomorrow, but that's all I can promise. However, as far as her cargo is concerned, I am extremely interested, and you know I pay well." He folded the document he had been reading and tucked it in his pocket. "Of course, you know I must compare this inventory with the one presented to the court before our agreement is finalized. I do appreciate the copy and your consideration. It is not that I do not trust you, but there are those who would attempt to take advantage."

The man across from him laughed. "Take advantage of Captain Durward? They'd have to be a fool to try."

Gabe inclined his head. "There are plenty of fools in this world." He had met several over the years. A few had attempted to take advantage of him. One or two had succeeded, but they would not be trying to do so again. He had made certain of that.

"Tomorrow?" his companion asked.

Gabe nodded.

"Then I had best get back to the dancing." The man across from him rose and gave a small bow.

"Business at a ball?" Tom asked as he settled into the chair vacated by the gentleman to whom Gabe had been talking.

"Does one not come to balls to speculate on investments?" Gabe leaned back and smiled into his glass of port before taking a drink. "My investments are just more at home on the water than in a ballroom. However, they are still beautiful and wealthy ladies."

Tom shook his head. "They are ships, not ladies."

Gabe shrugged. "Perhaps to a land lover such as yourself. How's the leg?"

"It is only slightly painful. However, I am finding it grows stronger each day."

"I am glad to hear it. And did you find the lady with whom you needed to speak?" That was the whole reason Tom had attended this ball – to find some woman who had caused a disaster to unfold in his family through her scheming. He had told Gabe that he wished to learn a few things that would hopefully put his mind at ease.

Tom nodded as a small smile curled his lips. "I am at peace."

Gabe clapped him on the shoulder. That was excellent news. Gabe was anxious to see Tom finally find some sort of rest for his spirit.

He had met Tom at the docks in London about three years ago now. The fellow's family had an interest in Antigua, and Gabe had an interest in the goods their interest might supply for him. However, he had found more than just a means of making a few pounds in that meeting. He had found one of his best friends. Tom was not like the majority of the ton. He did not care where Gabe had earned his money or why his eyes were so dark.

He took another swallow of his port. For all the devil-may-care swagger that Tom Bertram portrayed, he was a sensitive soul who was accepting of many whom others might discard.

"You are completely finished attempting to be what you are not?" Gabe asked quietly.

Tom nodded. "As finished with it as you are with adventuring." He shrugged. "I think we have both found our lot in life."

"And made peace with it," Gabe added.

"Yes, finally. Thankfully for you, it did not take nearly dying to discover your path."

Gabe pulled in a deep breath and expelled it slowly. "I faced death more than once before I came to my senses. You were just quicker to cotton on than I." He swallowed the last of his port. "In fact, it was my father's death last year which firmly set my feet on English soil for good." He had not confessed that to anyone until now, and Tom looked surprised as Gabe expected he would. "My mother arrived while you were attempting to escape the cold clutches of the afterlife."

"You should write poetry," Tom teased.

"Who's to say I do not," Gabe returned with ease. "Death sounded too crass when speaking of a friend."

"Is your mother adjusting well?"

"As well as can be expected. My bill for heating will be significant until she adjusts to the lack of warmth in the air, and she is finding it challenging to look so different. However, all the gentlemen who I have had around to do business have been polite, which has helped." He sighed. "If I could tolerate India as my father did, I would take her back there." He shook his head. "But I am not a company man as he was. I wish to find my own way in life, and that does limit me."

"You also love this damp, cold climate," Tom added. "Not even those of us who have lived here all our lives find it as pleasant as you do. I must say that was the one thing I appreciated about Antigua. It was warm."

"Has your father..." he stopped as a vision of loveliness in a cream coloured gown with a deep wine-coloured over-dress entered the room on the arm of some gentleman. He probably knew who the chap was and could figure it out if he put his mind to it. However, he'd rather just admire the lady on what's his name's arm.

"No, he has not disposed of it yet," Tom answered the question that had only been half spoken. "Mansfield is still too dependent on the funds."

Gabe turned his attention back to his friend for a moment. "That is too bad," he muttered before looking in the direction of the lady who had captured his interest and, to his surprise, was approaching their table.

"Miss Crawford," Tom said as he pushed up from his seat to stand with Gabe at her arrival before them.

"Mr. Bertram," Mary said before turning to her escort and sending him away with a whispered word.

Tom moved to pull out a chair for her. "May I present my friend, Mr. Gabriel Durward."

"It is a pleasure to meet you, Mr. Durward."

"Gabe, this is Miss Mary Crawford."

Gabe bowed and extended a greeting before retaking his

seat. Miss Crawford looked a bit uneasy as if she wished to say something but was uncertain if she should.

"Was there something with which I could help you?" Tom asked her.

Mary's eyes shifted to Gabe and back.

"He knows most of my secrets, Miss Crawford." Tom motioned for Gabe to stay when he attempted to rise, which was satisfactory with him. He would not find it a hardship to sit here with the lovely Miss Crawford. He did not even need to be included in the conversation as just admiring her beauty would be a pleasure.

"I was thinking about what you said in the garden," she began.

Gabe attempted to keep his features from giving anything away, but one brow refused to listen and lifted slightly. So this was the lady Tom had been seeking? This vision of loveliness was the cause of so much strife in the Bertram family? Miss Crawford did not look capable of such to him, but then he had learned that a dangerous vessel did not always appear to be hazardous at first blush.

"And have you come to a conclusion?" Tom asked.

"I have."

"Are you accepting my challenge?"

For a moment, Gabe thought Miss Crawford was going to be ill. Whatever had Tom challenged her to do?

"I am." She blew out a breath. "But I do not know how. My brother," she glanced at Gabe uneasily again before dropping her voice lower and continuing, "Henry will not speak to me. I have driven him away."

Tears gathered in her eyes, but she resolutely blinked them away. She might appear to be soft and delicate, but in that moment, Gabe knew better. Miss Crawford was very much like Tom. She was a sensitive, seeking soul, floundering in the storm, trying to find her way to a safe harbour.

"I have already become what I feared. I just had not realized it until you pointed it out to me."

"What do you fear?" Gabe smiled at her when she turned startled eyes toward him. "I apologize. I do tend to be direct at times."

Tom laughed. "And excessively curious, but his intentions are good," he assured Mary. "However, I think I can answer that one for you." He looked at Gabe. "You've only been home for a short time, but have you heard of Admiral Crawford?"

Gabe's eyes grew wide. He had heard tales of the admiral's exploits from several sources. Some of the tales were of conquests made in war that had earned him a handsome fortune, but many of the stories of conquests had nothing to do with war but everything to do with his treatment of women.

"I see you have," Mary said. "He is my uncle. My brother and I were raised by him and his wife after our parents died."

"He was a talented sailor." Gabe could think of nothing else to say about the man that was polite.

"Yes, we can agree on that," Mary replied. "And we would also likely agree that he is not a particularly agreeable person."

Gabe shrugged. Not particularly agreeable seemed a bit too soft for a man such as the admiral about whom he had heard tell.

"I loathe him, Mr. Durward. I have for many years. And so, it pains me to realize that I have in some respects become like him."

Her gaze dropped to the table, and her cheeks flushed.

Tom scratched his cheek. "Go dance with my friend, and I will give some thought to how you might start afresh."

"I beg your pardon?" Shock suffused Mary's face.

"Are you already engaged for this dance?" Tom asked.

"No, but..."

"Then I see no reason you cannot drag Gabe away from business for a few minutes while I contemplate your dilemma."

"I have explained very little of it," Mary retorted.

Tom smiled and shook his head. "I think I know you better than you give me credit. It is my sister who is now divorced, is it not?"

Mary's brow furrowed, and her eyes narrowed.

"I am not saying that to condemn you. I know from our

discussion earlier that you acted without a thought about the results. I was listening. However, you must acknowledge that I might be able to think about your predicament without further explanation." He shrugged. "And I have read the account in the paper about the confrontation with your brother and Lady St. James."

"That was you?" Gabe asked.

"Yes," Mary said with some force. "That was me. I am the horrid person who treated her brother badly because she felt a need to please her friends." Her eyes grew wide, and her hand flew to cover her mouth.

"Congratulations, Gabe. I do not think I have ever seen Miss Crawford unsettled."

"I apologize," Gabe offered. "That was not my intent."

Tom leaned forward. "Truly, Miss Crawford, I intend to help you if I can, but I will need some time to think." He looked at Gabe. "You have no other meetings arranged for this evening, do you?"

"No, one business meeting per soiree is my standard allotment." He rose from his seat. "I would be honored if you would allow me the privilege of dancing with you, Miss Crawford." He held up a finger and turned to Tom. "Do I need to approach her chaperone first?"

Tom shook his head and chuckled. "If you were to come to these soirees with more than business on your mind, you might be able to retain the rules of polite society more easily."

If there were more enchanting creatures like Miss Crawford at these soirees, Gabe would gladly come to them without conducting business. Unlike most of the ladies he had met at soirees, Miss Crawford was interesting. There were secrets that lay behind her dark eyes, and that enticed him.

"No," Tom continued, "I am a friend and have made the proper introductions. I believe you will not be chastised by Mrs. Grant."

"My sister," Mary offered when Gabe looked between them in confusion. "She has accompanied me tonight."

"Well, then, if I am not being improper, will you dance with me?" He extended his hand to her.

"Yes," she replied with a smile as she placed her hand in his, "I will dance with you."

Chapter 3

Mary took her place across from Mr. Durward. So far this season, this was the first set of dances that she would dance with someone to whom she had only just been introduced. Or, at least, it would be the first set of dances she had danced with a new acquaintance who was not married. Sarah, Lady St. James, was often introducing her to gentlemen, but rarely single gentlemen. They were almost always married and looking to present themselves as desirable to more ladies than just their wives. Oh! She was no better than the admiral's mistress, Fredricka! Mary might not warm the beds of any of the gentlemen with whom she danced, but she did nothing to encourage them to treat their wives with respect.

She closed her eyes against the spinning of the room and the churning of her stomach. This was at the same time both the worst and the best ball she had ever attended. It was horrible for all the times she was being reminded of the admiral in comparison to herself, but it was wonderful that she could see herself for who she had become because without that knowledge she knew that no change would be possible. How she would change — well, that was still not decided.

"Are you well, Miss Crawford?"

Mary opened her eyes and smiled into the deep brown, concerned eyes of the gentleman across from her. "I have not been feeling quite myself this evening," she admitted.

"Do you wish to sit out? I am happy to do so. Your wish is my command."

She shook her head. "I am certain when the music begins, I will be so distracted that I will not have a moment to consider my spinning head."

Gabe tipped his head and studied her closely. "I do not believe that is a good idea."

Mary did not turn her head, but her eyes shifted to look at the gentlemen on either side of Gabe. It did not appear as if they were listening to their conversation. "It is nothing more than my thoughts concerning what Mr. Bertram and I were talking about. I will be well."

"Are you certain?" Her partner's brow was furrowed, and he did not look at all convinced that she was well.

For a moment, Mary feared he would drag her from the line. She turned her most alluring smile on him – the one that worked on every man she had ever met. "I am certain."

The furrow between his eyes deepened. "I do not like it," he muttered. "But I will stay unless I see you stumble. Then, I will insist you leave the floor."

Her brows rose quite high. He seemed impervious to her smile. That was unusual.

"I should insist at present, but it will create too great a stir," he added.

She shivered slightly under his piercing gaze. He was a rather intense gentleman. "I know very little about you." She attempted to use that same smile again.

"That is because we have only just met."

Blast! He was still skewering her with that concerned expression. Would that the music would start!

"I have only been in London for five years now. Three completely, the two prior I was both here and not here, but then that is how it is for the captain of a ship, is it not?"

"You are a sailor?"

He nodded just as the music began. "Not in the navy. Privately. The captain of my own ship."

"You own a boat?" she asked as they joined hands for the first turn.

"I have funds tied up in several now, but five years ago, it was only one."

For several steps, they were separated. Then as they joined hands to proceed down the line, she asked, "Are you a harsh master?"

He shrugged. "I am a fair one. If at times that requires harshness, then I will be harsh. However, it is not my desire to be so."

They separated again. There was something in how Mr.

Durward spoke and the way his eyes watched her closely that told her he was not naturally harsh. Indeed, if he were close friends with Tom Bertram, he could not be excessively severe. That would be too reminiscent to Tom of his father, and she knew that Tom and his father mixed about as well as oil and water. That was something to recommend Mr. Durward to her. The admiral was harsh and not always because he had to be. Sometimes it was simply because he enjoyed seeing people scurry before him.

"You are not a landed gentleman then?" she asked at their next meeting of hands.

He shook his head. "Never intend to be, but one never knows. I am yet young. I have little besides myself and my business of which to think."

"Mr. Bertram seemed to hint that you think of your business a great deal."

"I do."

Two words? That was very little information. "Why?"

"Because it is my business and the source of my livelihood."

That was a slightly better explanation. She would have to be satisfied with it, she supposed, as they were once again separated.

"I like it," he added when they next met. "I cannot imagine being idle."

The gentleman next to him leaned toward him. "I hear there is a prize in the harbour."

Gabe patted the breast of his jacket. "I have a list of her contents right here, and I understand the court will hear the case in two days."

"You are intent on purchasing it?"

Gabe nodded. "The contents are worthy."

Mary listened with interest as they wove in and out and around.

The same gentleman continued, "Was it one of yours which took her?"

Gabe shook his head. "Not this time."

"A privateer?" The question flew from Mary's mouth as quickly as her brows rose in surprise.

Gabe gave a sharp nod of his head. "It's my way of defending against the enemy's success."

"While promoting his own," the man next to him laughed.

"Not unlike what the naval men do. However, I try never to sink my opponent."

"Oh, I am not faulting you," the gentleman hurried to assure him before they were separated to take a different place in the line and hear the last few notes of the music fade.

"Do you not approve of such activity?" Mr. Durward asked Mary as they formed a circle for the second dance of their set.

"I have never really considered it," she answered honestly. "I guess I just thought that the men who did such work were," she paused, "less refined."

He smiled at her whispered final words. "You are likely correct. I find all of this rather taxing at times. But, I would, at some point, like to marry, so it must be endured."

She returned his smile. He was delightfully refreshing from the gentlemen with whom she was usually partnered. They were constantly attempting to be what they were not as they crowed their delight about one dance or another. It was part of the game — the dreadfully, boring game in which she found herself ensconced.

"And you, Miss Crawford? Do you enjoy this?" He waved his hand to indicate the room.

She looked around her. What did she enjoy about this? It was not the posturing of the people. It was not the heat that increased with each dance. It was not the endless list of rules to be observed. Nor was it smiling when she wished to be serious.

"I enjoy dancing," she said at last, "but otherwise?" She lifted and lowered her shoulders in a shrug as a smile which was not forced or intended to entice or cajole curled her lips. "Not a thing. Not a single thing."

"Well, Miss Crawford," Gabe replied, "then we shall have to endure it together."

She took his hand as they began the dance. "I should like that very much, Mr. Durward."

~*~*

"Miss Crawford," Lady St. James approached Mary and Gabe as they took a turn around the ballroom before returning to where Tom awaited them in the card room. "I have heard the most interesting news." She gave Gabe an appraising look, allowing her eyes to roam from his face to his feet and back. "And who might this dark and daring looking gentleman be?"

"Lady St. James, this is Mr. Durward. He is a friend of a friend. Mr. Durward, this is Lady St. James."

"Durward? I am unfamiliar with the name." She tapped her fan on her hand. "Are you in parliament?"

"No, my lady."

"Do you have an estate in Kent?"

"No, my lady. I am in trade. My father was with the company, but I have set myself up."

Lady St. James's eyes grew wide, and she looked at Mary with concern. "Trade, you say?"

"Yes, my lady."

There was a firmness to Mr. Durward's jaw and a defiant look in his eyes. Mary could well imagine that he had met with many who responded in such a snobbish fashion.

"Oh, this will not do, Mary," Lady St. James said in a non-discreet whisper.

"What will not do?" Mary asked, feigning ignorance.

"My husband has standards," Lady St. James said with a tip of her head and a pleading look in her eyes.

Gabe leaned toward them. "I do not intend to be your

husband's mistress, so he has very little reason to assess whether I meet his standards or not," he whispered in the same non-discreet fashion Lady St. James had used. "Miss Crawford, do you care to continue to the card room or would you prefer that I leave you with Lady St. James and extend your regrets to Mr. Bertram?"

Lady St. James gasped twice — first at Gabe's comment about her husband's mistress and then at the name Mr. Bertram. "So, it is true? You have been with Mr. Bertram this evening?"

Mary pulled her eyes from Gabe's stern expression. There was no mistaking that he had been affronted and that he was indeed capable of being harsh when necessary. "Yes, my lady, and I am afraid I am engaged to Mr. Bertram for this next set. So, if you would excuse me."

"In the card room?" Lady St. James said with a laugh.

"His leg prevents him from dancing every set," Mary explained.

"That is now two sets you have spent with him. Are you attempting to snare the elder brother to punish the younger one?"

Mary shook her head. "No! I am not attempting to snare anyone. I am simply renewing acquaintances and forming new ones." She smiled at Gabe.

"New ones?" Lady St. James lifted her chin. "Such things might cost you your old ones."

Though it was hidden behind a sweet tone, Mary did

not miss the venom in her friend's words. Continuing on to the card room with Mr. Durward was a dangerous proposition. However, it could not be avoided, for Mary had no desire to remain as she had always been, and she quite liked Mr. Durward. He seemed open, honest, and interesting, and she would not mind being his friend even if it did cost her her old friends.

"It has been a pleasure, my lady. I do hope we meet again." She turned to Mr. Durward. "We should not keep Mr. Bertram waiting."

With determined steps and her head held high as she shuddered within, she allowed Mr. Durward to guide her from the room.

"Well done, Miss Crawford," he whispered. "That was a valiant first step in making a fresh start."

Mary shook her head. "Valiant it may be, but I am uncertain if it was wise."

He patted the hand that lay on his arm. "We are never certain of the wisdom of a thing such as this until we are well into it, and even then, as the smoke from the cannons swirls in the sky, we may waver and distrust what we know to be right. Stand strong, Miss Crawford. It is the only way to take the prize."

"Will you stand with me?" Mary asked. "I will need some friends."

Gabe pulled out a chair for her to have a seat. "With pleasure, Miss Crawford. With pleasure. However, you should know that I am prone to giving orders, so do not be offended if I occasionally present advice as a command."

Tom chuckled. "He did not rise to the positions he did without knowing how to give orders, and it seems it has either become part of his fabric or he was always thus. Now, tell me, why you will need friends to stand with you, Miss Crawford." He leaned forward eagerly.

"She has set her course without your guidance," Gabe replied.

To Mary, there was a hint of pride in Mr. Durward's tone, which was excessively pleasing. How long had it been since someone had been proud of her? "Lady St. James was not pleased to see me with a mere mister."

"From trade," Gabe added.

"You told her you were in trade?" Tom asked in surprise.

Gabe shrugged. "She was rude."

Tom rolled his eyes. "She has a Lady before her name. Of course, she was rude."

"I do not approve of rudeness. I will not accept it from those under my command, nor will I tolerate it with any amount of complacence when it is whispered in front of me in such a fashion as to pretend I am not there while guaranteeing I know what is being said."

Tom shook his head. "You will have a very hard time finding a wife with such an attitude. Word of a snub of Lady St. James will spread like fire did through London in

1666, and it could be just as damaging. Rebuilding will not be easy or quick. Ouch! I see no need to kick me."

"I do."

Mary blew out a breath. She had just ruined herself. How was she to find acceptance and a husband of any worth if she were to be shunned? She knew very well how vicious Sarah could be.

"Miss Crawford, the cannons will run their course and when the smoke clears you will have your prize. Do you know what that prize is?" He shot an angry glare at Tom while speaking gently to her.

She shook her head.

He took her hand. "You will have destroyed the admiral."

Mary blinked.

"You will have destroyed the admiral," Gabe repeated.

She nodded, a skitter of excitement danced up her arms, causing them to shiver. She would like nothing better than to destroy every trace of the admiral who had found his way into her behavior.

"We," he shot another glare at Tom, "will not let you take on water."

"Right," Tom agreed, looking rather sheepish now that he had caught on to why Gabe had kicked him. "I take it my plan is not needed?"

Mary shrugged.

"I was going to start by suggesting cutting ties with old acquaintances, but it seems you have already done so."

"And then, you were going to send her brother to visit her, were you not?" Gabe leveled a glare at Tom once again.

Tom shrugged. "I was?"

"Does he know where you are staying?" Gabe asked Mary.

"Oh, yes! I am staying with our sister and her husband."

He looked at Tom. "Go tell him."

"See what I told you. He is very good at giving orders." Tom stood and gave Gabe a salute. "I shall do my best to locate Mr. Crawford and deliver my message, Captain."

"Go away," Gabe said with a grin. "But return quickly," he called after him.

"You are very good friends," Mary said as he turned back toward her.

Gabe nodded. "We are. A bit of an odd mix – what with him being the next Sir Thomas and me just commanding ships."

Mary shook her head and chuckled. "I doubt very much that you are 'just commanding ships.' If I were a gambling woman, which I am at times, I would hazard a guess that you do more than own part of several ships. There is likely a warehouse that stores the goods from your boats as well as a fleet of merchants who come to you to buy those goods."

He smiled. "You would win that wager. Now, before my friend returns, I do not know where your sister and her husband, Mrs. Grant and –"

"Dr. Grant," she supplied. "He has a stall at Westminster."

"Indeed? How very happy for him."

"Both he and my sister are pleased."

"Are you pleased?"

Mary nodded her head. "I am. My sister is very loving. Dr. Grant is a bit of a bore, but he is kind. They deserve to be happy."

"And where do they live?" Gabe asked.

Mary took a calling card from her reticule and wrote the direction on the back of it.

Taking the card from her, Gabe slipped it into his pocket. "You shall have a call from at least one friend," he said with a wink. "And two if I can put Tom up to it."

"He does not have to call," Mary said quickly. "I am certain he would rather be rid of me."

Gabe tipped his head and looked at her for a long silent minute. Just as she was beginning to squirm, he said, "then you do not know the new Tom Bertram."

He shook his head as he opened her mouth to speak.

"You are worthy of his notice, Miss Crawford." He tapped his pocket. "As well as mine."

Chapter 4

Mary picked up her pen for the second time in three minutes only to return it once again to its holder.

"It is only an invitation," her sister, Margaret said, looking up from the book she was reading. "I can write it if you cannot."

Mary shook her head. "It must be from me. I have created the trouble between Henry and me, so it stands to reason that I should be the one to attempt the repair." She picked up her pen once again.

"He would not come call on us?"

"No, he would not."

Tom had attempted to persuade Henry to call on Mary, but even though Tom insisted that Mary was indeed ready to repent of her behaviour, Henry held fast to his position that if she were truly repentant, she would be the source of the invitation, not a friend. Mary had been a bit shocked that Henry had refused Tom. She had been confident that the surprise of being approached by Tom in a friendly fashion would have made Henry compliant. However, it had not. Henry had been gracious in welcoming Tom, and he had, according to Mr. Bertram, extended a very heartfelt apology for his behaviour in the affair affecting Tom's sister Maria. But he had been unyielding when it came to his own sister's poor behaviour.

Dearest Henry,
She began before contemplating how she should approach the subject of her guilt.

Henry knew all her schemes. To attempt anything other than being completely honest would only make him scoff and refuse yet again to see her. Therefore, when she applied her pen to the paper to continue, her thoughts would not arrange themselves neatly for there was no structure to the play. Indeed, there was no game afoot. There were only the contents of her heart to spill upon the page.

I cannot express to you just how great my sorrow is when I contemplate how I behaved toward the Bertrams. To have been party to the destruction of a marriage is reprehensible. I see that now, thanks to Mr. Bertram's conversation with me at the ball last night. However, that atrocity pales in comparison to how I have dealt with you, my dearest brother, whom you know I love better than anything in this world.

To have been the source of your sorrow with Fanny and then to have attempted to replicate that sorrow again with Miss Linton is unforgivable. Regardless of that fact, I would try to beg your forgiveness anyway as I miss you. So very greatly. It is as if a part of me has been removed. I truly thought that the removal of Edmund was the most profound sorrow I would feel from my actions, but it is not. While I am sure I could have loved Edmund and that I perhaps did, it is the loss of you which I regret the most. Oh, I fear I am rambling.

I do not know how to best express myself to you with paper and ink. Please, my dear brother, come to see me so that I might say these things to you in person. Our sitting room will be empty or nearly so, and I shall be at home every day this week, as I do not expect to have any friends left after last night's ball. I would rather not commit the details of that incident to paper as it would take a great deal of explaining as to who Mr. Durward is and why he should cause me to break ties with Sarah.

I know this is poorly written and jumbled, much as my mind is of late. I pray you would overlook the wandering thoughts and only see that I am truly repentant of all the sorrow I have caused you and wish only to see you again.

Margaret is also anxious for a call. Do not make us wait any longer.

Your loving, though sadly misguided, sister,

Mary

She read it once over, handed it to her sister to read, and then, having gotten Margaret's approval, she folded and sealed the missive.

"We will see it delivered at once." Margaret took the envelope from her and left to send someone to deliver it to Henry's house. When she returned, she did not come alone.

"Mr. Durward," Mary greeted with a smile. "It is delightful to see you."

"I am a man of my word, Miss Crawford."

"I do not doubt that, sir," she replied as she fiddled with the lace on the wrist of one sleeve. How did one entertain a friend from whom she did not require anything?

"Did you drive?" Margaret asked, sneaking a peek out the window. Margaret enjoyed carriages of all sorts, though curricles were her favorite.

"No, I rode," Mr. Durward replied. "The weather was ideal for it today, so one must take advantage of it when he can."

"Oh, indeed!" Margaret cried. "This time of year can be challenging for both man and beast. Why just the other day, Mary and I were going to take a tour of the park. We had planned for it all week, and then just as we were eating breakfast and making our final preparations, there was tap, tap, tapping at the window. Such cold rain it was, too. As you can imagine, we did not go to the park."

Much to Mary's surprise, Mr. Durward replied with "And what did you do instead?"

She had thought he would be disinterested in whether or not they had gone to the park, for he was a man of business, not leisure.

"I worked on a blanket while Mary played her harp. It was lovely and warm with the fire built up to take the dampness from the air. And then, we had tea just as we would have if there had been a full party even though it was just for the two of us."

"That sounds most pleasurable. Did you find it enjoyable, Miss Crawford?" He asked from where he was draped comfortably on the sofa.

"I will not lie. I was disappointed, but Margaret is so good at cheering me up."

"Do you like the harp, Mr. Durward?" Margaret asked.

He shrugged. "It is as fine an instrument as any, I suppose. However, I cannot say that I have listened to it very often."

Margaret placed a hand on Mary's arm. "Oh, Mary, you will have to play for Mr. Durward. She is most excellent, I assure you," she added to Mr. Durward.

"Perhaps another day," Mary replied. "Mr. Durward did not come to listen to music."

"I will admit that without a business plan before me, I have very little idea how to conduct myself in a sitting room. If you wish to play, Miss Crawford, you may."

Mary shook her head. "I think another time would be better." She would rather discover more about him than have him sitting silently while she played.

"Whatever you wish."

His eyes held hers. How could so much comfort be found in eyes that were so intently focused?

"Mary tells me that you were once a captain of a ship," Margaret said when neither Mary nor Mr. Durward continued speaking.

"I still am when needed," he replied with a smile. His eyes held Mary's for a moment longer before turning toward her sister. "However, I do try to make certain that I am not needed. I would not tell everyone this, but I have never preferred the sea to the land."

"You have not?" That was surprising. Most men who chose to go to sea spoke as if they were powerless to resist the call of the sea and adventure.

"Then why did you sail?" Margaret asked.

It was the question Mary also wished to have answered.

"That is a bit of a convoluted story but suffice it to say that the sea provided adventure and distance between my father and me." He grimaced. "A stupid notion formulated by a young mind who rebelled against the ideals of his father. Truly, my father was a good man. I was just far more independent and headstrong than I likely should have been."

"Should have been? Or are?" Mary asked in a light teasing tone. Mr. Durward appeared to be a very resolute indi-vidual. Had Tom not said as much last night?

Mr. Durward chuckled. "You are correct, Miss Craw-ford. I have not changed so much in essentials, but I have hopefully grown wiser and less foolish."

"Much like your friend, Mr. Bertram, seems to have done," Mary added.

Mr. Durward frowned as he nodded his agreement. "Tom was previously engaged today, or he would have called with me." His tone was apologetic.

"Think nothing of his absence," Mary said hastily. "I did not mention him because he is not here. I was simply not-ing the similarity between the two of you and noting the change I saw in him last night."

"He will call," Mr. Durward insisted.

"I am certain he will," Mary replied. "Please think noth-ing more of it. I am sorry I have brought him up at all."

Mr. Durward's eyes grew wide. "I did not mean to upset you with my comments," he rushed to assure her. "I merely wished you to know that you are, as I said last night, worthy of his notice." He leaned forward and skew-ered her again with one of his unsettlingly intense looks of concern. "I fear many have been less than trustworthy in your life – if Lady St. James and the admiral are any indica-tions — and I would not have you thinking that my friend or I would not prove to be honorable."

Trustworthy. That was a quality Mary longed to find in

someone. She had had it with Edmund and Fanny. Neither would have played her false. No, she thought, as remorse filled her, that job had been hers alone. She was the one preening and pretending.

"Thank you," she muttered with a small smile, "and I would say that I do not feel worthy of much of anything, but I fear either you or Margaret would scold me for saying it. So, I will not."

"I most certainly would scold you," Margaret replied.

"And I would say that one does not need to feel worthy to be worthy," said Mr. Durward.

"Did you see the prize ship?" Mary asked, turning the subject away from feelings of guilt and delight which when mingled as they were at present in her mind were decidedly discomposing.

"I did."

"And was it to your liking?"

"For the right price, it is." He smiled, a glimpse of teeth showing in the action. "I do think I will be adding her to my possessions, but she'll be for cargo and not plundering, and she'll likely be the last I add for some time. I will need to refit her and find a crew to sail her as well as garner some reasons to set her sails."

The confidence that radiated from his every action and word told Mary that this new ship would not stay in port for long after her refitting.

He tipped his head and looked at her inquisitively, as

if what he was about to ask her was of great importance. "Would you like to see her and the others? I could take you for a tour of the dock – all very politely done in a carriage so as not to soil your skirts and shoes."

"And your warehouse?" Mary asked. She had been wondering what treasures he might have stored away in a building somewhere near the docks.

"If you wish," he replied, a bright smile spreading across his face. "And in return, you can play something for me on your harp, and I shall listen most intently." He pushed up from where he had been sitting. "If I were you, I would wear something sturdy when we go on our tour. There are dust and dirt to be found, and the wind off the water can be cutting if the day is not bright."

"Oh, we do not mind a little chill," Margaret assured him. "As long as it is not raining."

"Yes, yes, to attempt a tour in the rain would be dreadful," he agreed. "I will not be able to call tomorrow as there are some business matters to which I must attend, but perhaps the day after that, I can collect you and take you for a tour."

Mary opened her mouth to eagerly accept his invitation but then closed it again.

"Is something amiss?" he asked her.

"I just sent my brother a letter saying I would be home all week. I cannot risk being away if he should call."

"Then, our tour will wait until next week. I would never wish to be the cause of you not keeping your word."

He was entirely too good she thought as he said his good days and took his leave.

"His skin is such a lovely brown colour without being at all creased," Margaret muttered when he was gone. She had said the same thing last night after meeting him. "He really is handsome."

Mary would not refute the statements. Mr. Durward was a darkly handsome fellow. "He seems very nice."

"Most pleasant. Most pleasant," Margaret agreed. "Now, will you be playing for me, or would you like to continue working on the baby clothes for the foundling's hospital?"

"The clothes," Mary replied, settling into a chair at the work table while her sister got out the workbasket.

Chapter 5

Gabe swung up onto his horse and took a look back at the door to the Grants' home. He had never thought to meet a lady of quality who would be interested in seeing his ships and storehouse. He had concluded that if, by some good fortune, he should find a lady to accept him with his ties to trade and his complexion that was naturally darker than that of most gentlemen in England who had not been put to sea or left to work in a field all day, one of two things would be true about that lady. Either she would be desperate for a good match due to some deficit in her own appearance or family, or she'd be only too happy to spend all of his money on some fancy home far removed from whatever it was that he did. Not that she would ever truly know what it was as she would never wish to know.

However, Miss Crawford did not appear to be such a lady. She was undeniably beautiful. Her hair and eyes were not quite so dark as his, and her skin was the colour of fresh cream with just a touch of tea added. Her figure was just as he preferred. To look at her, she was perfection, and he would not deny that her beauty enticed him. Yet, there was something more about her that drew him – a familiar uncertainty of being part of something and yet not. It was that same shifting, searching soul that had driven him to the sea and Tom to horseraces and the theatre.

For some, no matter how good their lots in life were, there was a struggle, deep and disquieting, that had to be faced when it came to finding their purpose and place. To have been such a person in the home of Admiral Crawford must have been challenging indeed. If the stories Gabe had heard were true, and he had no reason to believe they were not, the admiral was not one to take prodigious care of anything save his ship and himself. Gabe had heard the tales about the number of mistresses the admiral had had. It was not something he hid from anyone, not even his wife.

Gabe nudged his horse forward.

To be a young woman under such care and to see her aunt treated with so little respect must have taken its toll. But, then, just as he and Tom had done, Mary had found acceptance and a place to be something. It was just not a proper something.

Tom had found friends who allowed, even encouraged, him to run headlong into ruin, and it had almost killed him. Gabe himself had found acceptance in the ranks on an East Indiaman. The life on board had called to him. It had promised him adventure and a place to develop his skills of command. And it had delivered on both accounts. It had also nearly cost him his life on more than one occasion.

While standing on the beach of a tropical island at the end of a successful skirmish that had left Gabe with a small hole in his upper arm and had once again lined the pockets of the company, Gabe had come to the realization that where he thought he belonged and how he thought he could please his father while still pleasing himself was an illusion. It was not who he was. It was not where he belonged. On that beach as the waves lapped the sand, he had determined that he did not wish to continue his contribution to a company that seemed to be growing more and more hungry for power and seemed to have less and less respect for the people whose lands they conquered. People like his mother.

His father had not been willing to leave his position. He had been in it for too many years. He had nothing to return to in England and not enough years left to strike out on his own. Added to that, he was not so disgruntled with company behaviour as Gabe was. His father had called Gabe's ideas "foolish alarmist views of the young."

It had been a painful day when Gabe had set sail for England, never to return to India. Thankfully, both his father and his mother had written to him, and, to the welcome balm of his soul, his mother's letters always contained some mention of his father's pride in Gabe's successes. He sighed as his home came into view. If only his father had been the sort of man to say such things himself, it would have given them the weight that only the voice of a father to a son could.

These were the thoughts which kept Gabe company on his journey home and would have continued to fill his mind had he been entering an empty house, but his home was not empty. And so, his ruminations about the past were put aside to be picked up again some other time. Presently, there was another woman who deserved, and to whom he would give, his attention.

"Welcome home, my son," his mother lifted onto her toes to greet him with a kiss when he entered the hall. There had been a time when he had needed to stretch to meet her cheek, but that was many years ago now. She was still as short as she ever was, but he had inherited his father's height with interest.

"You do not have to wait for me by the door, Mama."

She seemed to always be right here, waiting to greet him when he returned from some outing – even when the hour was late, and she should be in bed.

"I was not. I was waiting in the sitting room." She winked and wrapped her arm around his. "You are so cold."

"I am not cold."

She was always cold. He was not.

"Come. Sit by the fire and tell me about your lady."

"She is not my lady, Mama." He would like her to be, but as of yet, Miss Crawford was not.

He settled into a chair near the window and not the fire. The heat of India was not something he missed. He had been born into it, but it was not something he craved as some did.

"How can she not be? You are so handsome, just like your father. Can you not make a bargain with her brother?"

"That is not exactly how it is done here, Mama. And you know I wish to have a wife who has chosen me as much as I have chosen her." He had discussed that fact with her many, many times over the years.

His mother sighed and took up her knitting. "I just want you to be as happy as I was with your father, and I would not mind having a daughter to talk to, you know."

"Yes, Mama, I know."

"So tell me about your Miss Crawford."

Gabe sighed. There would be no putting her off. For though small in stature, his mother was not short on determination. He smiled. That was something she and Miss Crawford shared. It was also likely why he could not abide a simpering milquetoast maid for longer than one dance. His grandmother, his mother's mother, had been the same. Small and unassuming but solid as iron when needed. And both had married successful company men.

"She wishes to see my boats."

His mother looked up from her knitting in surprise. "She does not wish to sail on them, does she? I can tell her that while it might seem like an adventure for the first few hours, it soon grows dull."

Gabe chuckled. "You do not wish to take a trip with me to some exotic location?"

Her eyes sparkled. "Ireland would be acceptable. I think we could reach it before I became too bored."

"Ireland is not exotic," Gabe protested.

"It is to a girl from India," she replied. "Why if I had grown up here, India would be exotic, but as I was not born here, India is but common – pleasantly warm, but common."

"Point taken," he replied. "I do not think Miss Crawford wishes to sail away on one of my ships, but she is curious about them."

"And this makes you happy?"

Gabe nodded. "I like her very much, Mama."

His mother smiled. "It takes very little for one's heart to decide its course. That is how it was for your father and me. I saw him once before we married and that was enough. I knew that I was not being given away in vain. My heart, as well as my father, would be happy." She glanced up at him. "Do not give me that look. It was how things were done at the time — one man tying himself to another in some agreement by taking a bride."

"I dislike thinking of you as a payment."

She shook her head. "I was not a payment, my son. I was a reward. Your father said it often." She sighed. "I wish he could see you now. He would be so proud of you."

"I wish he could see me now as well. You are not alone in missing him. I have just had more years to grow accustomed to the absence. And before you say it, I know that it was of my own doing, but I will tell you once again, I could do naught else."

She placed her knitting in her lap. "Strong men are not easy men. Does your Miss Crawford know this?"

Gabe blew out a breath. "I do not know if she does."

Mary knew about oppressive men, but he doubted she truly understood what a strong man was.

"I do not believe she trusts men. There have been few in her life who have been worthy of her good opinion."

Sadness spread across his mother's face. "She is strong then?"

"Yes, she has had to be, and I believe her heart is good." He paused and drew a deep breath which he released slowly. He hoped that her heart was not so locked away and unused to kindness that it would prove to be too difficult to convince her that he was not like other men and that he could be trusted.

"You are worried for her?"

Gabe nodded.

"Then you love her already."

It was not a question, but a statement of fact spoken in

a tone that told Gabe she would hear no refute if he were to make one, which he wasn't. He was quite sure that his mother was correct. There was just something about Miss Crawford that captivated him.

"Is she pretty?" his mother asked.

Gabe smiled.

"I can see that she is."

"She has dark hair and eyes and a creamy complexion. She is taller than you, and," he winked at her, "she has a few more curves than you do."

"You are not to notice your mother's lack of curves," she said with a laugh.

"I was only making a comparison for description purposes," he replied.

Her brows rose over twinkling eyes. "I do hope those curves are in all the proper places," she said in as proper a tone as she could muster. She had always been able to play the part of a proper lady. She had been trained in all the same accomplishments as any other English lady had been. Her father had insisted that she become as British as possible despite her brown complexion, for he intended for her to marry not from her country but from his. However, she had a playfulness to her that often liked to thwart propriety when in private.

"Precisely where they should be," Gabe replied with a grin.

"Does she know about me?"

Gabe shook his head. "Not yet, but I am certain she will not object."

"If she does, I can always be sent back to India," she said over the click of her knitting needles.

"You cannot be. You are my mother, and I will not be tossing you out. If she does not love you, she cannot love me."

"I only wish for you to be happy," his mother said softly. "I would not stand in the way of that."

"And you will not. For I shall not be happy with any woman, who cannot accept that you are my mother."

His mother shrugged. "Her friends may not be best pleased."

"I believe she has very few true friends, Mama. Fitting into the right circles is not easy or pleasant and does not make for many lasting friendships." Once again, he released a great sigh. "She has very few, if any, of those so-called friends left because she chose to be my friend. She will not object to you."

The sparkle in his mother's eyes had been replaced with a shimmer of unshed tears, but her smile had only grown. "And who would not choose you, my angel."

He shook his head as he pushed up from his place. "I have a few things to see to before dinner." He cupped her face in his hand and kissed her forehead. "I shall bring her around to meet you as soon as I am able. Currently, she is waiting to heal a breach with her brother, but as soon as she is available, I will invite her to visit you." He kissed her forehead once again. "You are the best decision my father ever made."

"I most certainly am," she replied before shooing him away and reminding him not to be late for dinner.

Chapter 6

Mary sat at the worktable in the sitting room with the infant's gown for the foundling hospital. She was nearly finished with it. It needed only a few more embellishments, something to make it pretty, for, in Mary's opinion, even those in need should be surrounded by small bits of beauty when possible, even if those bits of loveliness were merely small white flowers stitched on white fabric.

It had been two days since she had last seen anyone other than a few of her sister's friends. The lack of callers had provided her with ample time to stitch and read. However, being nearly friendless was frightfully dull, and Mary had prepared herself to be just as bored today. So, it surprised her when the housekeeper entered with someone who was calling specifically for her.

"Henry!" she cried in delight.

"Mary."

He was smiling. This was good. There was a hope that they could restore their friendship.

"Please, please, be seated. I will see that tea is brought

straightaway," said Margaret. She stopped long enough to squeeze Henry's hand and tell him how happy she was to see him before she scooted from the room.

Mary finished the stitch she had started before her brother had entered. Then she lay her work aside and took a seat near him. After sitting down, she smoothed her skirts uneasily. How did one start a conversation such as this?

"I was pleased to get your letter," Henry said.

"I meant every word," Mary assured him. "I know I do not deserve your forgiveness. I have been abominable."

He placed a hand on hers. "Tell me about Mr. Durward."

Mary blinked. She had not expected that. "I know very little really. Let me see. He is a friend of Tom Bertram, and he has several ships and a warehouse."

"He is a merchant then?"

Mary nodded. "He has privateers, but I think he also has other sorts of ships that just carry on regular trade. I believe, he is working on securing a prize ship and her cargo today. I know it was soon to come before the prize court."

"He is an industrious fellow, then?"

"Oh, very. He was even conducting business at the last ball I attended."

It was indeed her last ball. She doubted she would be invited to many now, and she was positive that to attend a public ball would be painful for some time.

"Would that be the ball at which Mr. Edwards spoke to you?"

Mary swallowed and nodded. "I have not been to any others."

"You were looking for me there."

"I was."

"Why?"

She shrugged. "I missed you, and I grew tired of my friends."

"Tired enough of them to pass them over in favour of new friends?"

He was looking at her in a very intense fashion, which was so unlike the Henry she remembered. The old Henry had always been amiable and far too willing to please both her and himself. The old Henry was rarely serious about anything.

"Yes." She clasped the hand that held hers between both of her hands. "Mr. Bertram found me after Mr. Edwards had, and what Mr. Bertram had to say left me with no choice but to walk away from all I have ever known. Oh, Henry, I have been such a fool – an arrogant, self-serving, fool – very much like our uncle always was. I will not be like him, Henry. I will not. Even if I do not know how to be anything else, I must attempt to be different."

"Then you have found your heart?"

"Yes. I most certainly have."

A smile graced his face as a sigh escaped him. "I had thought you had when I heard the rumors about you snubbing Lady St. James in favour of some gentleman in trade. Mr. Durward, is it?"

"I am sure all of London has heard about that! Sarah is not one to keep such things to herself."

"At least it was not in the paper."

"How can you ever forgive me!"

"You are my sister," he answered in a serious tone, "and I know from your letter and what happened at that ball that you are indeed repentant. However, there is the matter of Miss Linton. You must treat her with the utmost respect if you are to retain my friendship."

Tears threatened to fall, and for a moment Mary considered allowing them. It would be acceptable to appear weak before her brother. She knew he would not use her weakness against her. However, some habits do not die easily, and so she resolutely denied herself the liberty of tears until later when she could conceal them from view in her room. "I feel my sin most grievously," she assured him.

"You can bring her to dinner one evening," Margaret, who had entered with the tea service during their discussion, suggested. "I would be very pleased to meet her." She turned to Mary. "And we can invite Mr. Durward as well, so that Henry can meet him. He is very handsome," she added to Henry.

"Are you still attempting to marry our sister off to

whomever you find to be pleasing?" Henry asked with a laugh.

"Oh, yes! And I would be doing the same for you if you had not already found yourself a happy situation." She made short work of pouring the tea and inviting them to join her at the table as she moved all their work aside to the window seat. "Mary is almost finished with a gown for the foundling's hospital."

For the second time in not many more days, Mary heard someone speak of her with pride. It was a wonderful feeling.

"Our sister came home just... When was it?" Margaret paused and thought for a moment. "Oh, it does not matter when it was. Some days ago, Mary came home with some story about Mr. Edwards doing work at a charity and how he seemed happy much like you were. Anyway, the end of the story is that she thought perhaps she would attempt some charity work herself to see what it was like, and I do think she has found it satisfying so far, though she has only made the one gown. There has not been time for more than that."

"I am impressed, and Mr. Edwards and Miss Barrett will be pleased to hear it when Charles returns. I have to admit that I never expected to see him so interested in charitable work, but then Miss Barrett is persuasive."

"Where has he gone?" Margaret asked.

"I am not supposed to say, but he has gone to speak with Mr. Barrett."

"He plans to marry Miss Barrett, then?" Mary asked as she placed a shortbread on her plate.

"If he can get both her father's and her permission," Henry replied with a chuckle, "which a gentleman with his reputation may find challenging. However, if anyone can charm both a father and his daughter, it is Edwards."

Mary shook her head. "How odd this season has been. First, there is you finding a proper young lady and becoming respectable."

"Which I must say is about time," Margaret inserted, and Henry agreed.

"And then there is Mr. Edwards," Mary added, "who was worse than you for charming the ladies, becoming a whatever it is he is becoming. I know it is not what he has been."

"And now there is you, cutting ties with your friends. Will we be adding Mr. Durward to our family?"

Henry wore his familiar teasing smile. It was a welcome sight to Mary. How she had missed him!

"We have only just met," she replied.

"And how long were we at Mansfield before you had selected a husband?"

Mary glared at him through narrowed eyes. "We both know how that worked out, do we not? I think it best if I do not select a husband in such haste this time." She sighed.

"By the by, Tom assures me that Edmund and I would not suit."

"And what is your opinion?" Henry asked.

"Since his injury and illness, it would appear that Mr. Bertram has developed an annoying habit of being right because I have to agree with him. I would have grown bored. Edmund would not have changed. He was what he was, and he was happy being such. I likely would have been miserable because I am not Margaret. I am not made to be a parson's wife. And my unhappiness would have made Edmund miserable in return. You know how petulant I can be."

Henry laughed. "Indeed, I do." He blew out a breath. "We both learned something from our time at Mansfield, did we not? Painful though the lessons were."

Mary nodded, although she was not certain she had actually learned anything until recently when finally, she had been made to view her actions for what they were while walking in the garden with Tom. She had known that what she had done was not best, but she had not fully considered just how wrongly she had acted until the admiral was held up before her as a mirror of her own behaviour.

"Now, about this Mr. Durward, Margaret. Do you think we have a hope of seeing our sister settled?"

Mary swatted his arm, but she could not be displeased. She had missed Henry's teasing, and if Mr. Durward proved to be as trustworthy as he claimed, she would not mind being his wife. So, beyond the swat of Henry's arm, she said nothing, choosing instead to apply herself to her tea while she listened to her sister and brother conjecture about her future until another very welcome caller arrived.

"It is a pleasure to meet you," Henry said as they all took their seats once again after Margaret had made all the proper introductions. "My sisters tell me you are in trade."

"Indeed, I am. I have an import and export business as well as dealings with some financing of projects."

"Then you are doing well?"

Mary wanted to sink into her chair so that she could not be seen. Since when did her brother start asking such questions of the gentlemen she entertained as possible suitors?

"Some would say so."

Taking note of the smile Gabe wore, Mary breathed a sigh of relief that he had not been offended by the question. That was also strange. Since when did she concern herself with whether Henry offended anyone with his behaviour? Had not both she and he lived for the pleasure of unsettling the occasional person?

"I have promised a tour of my operation to your sisters," Gabe continued. "I do hope that is to your satisfaction."

Henry nodded. "I see no reason to oppose such an outing."

Gabe leaned forward, his elbows resting on the arms of

the chair, and his fingers lacing in front of him. "Since you are here, and I am not certain when we shall have a chance for a bit of conversation in the future as I have no intention of returning to any social events for some time..."

"You do not?" Margaret asked in surprise.

Gabe shook his head. "I did not like Lady St. James, and I am equally as certain she did not like me. I shall let the dust of our meeting settle before I expose myself to her censure and likely cause another stir when she provokes me beyond my limits once again."

"She was most certainly displeased," Henry acknowledged. "I have heard the whispers."

Gabe acknowledged the comment with a nod. "I am not unaccustomed to such things. I am in trade, after all, and not so refined as some." Again, he wore a very pleasing smile that spoke of the truth of his words. He seemed at ease with not being fully accepted and did not appear to care what society thought of him.

"Now," he continued, his smile fading somewhat but not completely.

He was charming, Mary thought with a silent sigh.

"To get to what I wished to discuss with you. I am a man of business, and I like to know in advance to whom I should speak regarding agreements. I know that you and Miss Crawford lived with your uncle, but neither of you do any longer. Therefore, should the admiration I have for your sister flourish into something that seems to be lasting, should I call on you or the admiral — or Dr. Grant because she is residing with him."

Mary's eyes grew wide. She had only just met Mr. Durward, and he was thinking of marriage? She had not even had time to make her desires known to him. She smiled. He was choosing her without persuasion of any sort. It was a novel feeling.

Henry grimaced. "She was handed over to me by the admiral when we left him."

"It was an ugly scene?" Gabe inquired.

"Nothing was ever pleasant with the admiral," Mary answered.

Henry shook his head. "What he said was reprehensible. Even in my former iteration, I knew it to be."

Mary lifted her chin and pushed down the hurt that rose as she remembered her uncle's words. "He had no use for housing a lady who could not possibly repay him in any satisfactory fashion."

"He said that?" Margaret cried. "You never told me that."

"I could not," Mary answered softly. It hurt her to be so easily discarded then, and the pain of such a thing had not faded in the time she had been away from him. It should not have surprised her that he cared so little for her since he was so unfeeling toward his own wife, but it did.

Gabe wore the same expression as the one Mary had seen him wear when addressing Lady St. James. He was offended, and her heart thrilled a small amount as she realized that, presently, he was not offended on his own account but on her behalf. Perhaps. Just perhaps, she had found a gentleman whom she could trust with her heart.

"I will not say what I think of such a man while in polite company." Gabe shook his head and blew out a breath as if struggling to contain his displeasure. Then, he smiled a small, kind smile at Mary and said, "I am very sorry you had to endure that. No lady should be so treated."

Mary ducked her head as she thanked him. If she kept looking at his earnest, concerned-filled dark eyes, she would not be able to keep her tears where they belonged.

Had she ever felt so treasured? She was positive she never had. She could easily lose her heart to Mr. Durward, but she mustn't. Not yet. Not until she knew that she could trust him completely. She would not willingly present her heart to any gentleman, no matter how kind and charming he appeared, and allow it to be crushed.

"Then if or when the time should come, I will call on you," Gabe said to Henry.

"I would appreciate that," Henry replied. "However, I am certain Dr. Grant's permission could be sought in my stead. He would not let any harm come to my sister. Of that, I am certain." Henry shifted positions, becoming even more comfortably positioned. "Now, tell me about you. I have heard that you have only lived in England for a few years."

Gabe nodded. "I was born in India and lived there my entire life until I set foot on that first company ship. Then, my world expanded, and I was given the opportunity to see many places, including London."

"And of all the places you saw, you chose to live here?" Henry asked. "I would think that there would be many more interesting places in the world in which to take up residence than London."

Gabe shook his head. "I took one look at her on that first foggy, dreary day and knew I would return. I could have chosen another colony in which to set up my business, but no other port spoke to me as this one did." He shrugged. "I do not know why exactly. Perhaps it was because the company is here, and so I wished to position myself as one of its rivals set to take up what I believe it is destined to lose at some point in the none too distant future. Perhaps it was something else – the history, the architecture, the vibrance, or the idea that the heart of the empire beats from here. It could have been a dozen reasons I suppose. I have not paused to ferret them out. I only know that by the end of the short time that I was here, I knew I would come back. This was where I was meant to be."

"Do you always make such quick decisions?" Margaret asked.

Gabe shook his head. "Not always, but I do not attempt to take too long in deliberations either. If one is not quick to decide things, one might lose out on a very profitable venture or place his money where it cannot possibly make him a return." He chuckled. "I sound like a rather boring old fellow. Tom tells me I need to find something other than business upon which to think. I have always thought he was wrong, but I am not so certain any longer."

"Have you been to the theatre?" Henry asked.

"No, I have not been. Tom has managed to get me to attend various soirees, and I do enjoy touring the museum and the occasional ride through a park, but I must admit I have not attended a play – though I have read a great number of them."

"Then, I will secure an invitation for you and Mary to join myself and some friends one night."

Mary shook her head. He could not mean she was to attend a play with Miss Linton.

"Miss Linton is a forgiving sort of lady," Henry assured her before she had even spoken. "Mrs. Kendrick, Mrs. Barrett, and Mr. Linton might be less so, but is it not right that you prove yourself changed to them?"

Sit in a box with people toward whom she had behaved so dreadfully? The thought was perhaps the most terrifying one Mary had ever had to ponder. Mr. Edwards had been so cutting in his remarks to her at that ball. She was not entirely sure she was up to the playing such a role.

"I would be delighted to join you if Miss Crawford will join me."

Mary knew that Mr. Durward could see the fear she felt

when she looked at him in surprise for his eyes were filled with concern.

"Please," he said softly. "I shall not let you take on water, Miss Crawford."

Mary sucked in a breath and expelled it. How could she do anything other than grant him his wish when he was so gallantly offering his protection while looking at her with that intense, caring expression that caused her to shiver. "Very well. I shall do my penance."

Her agreement settled the matter, and it was decided that soon, perhaps in a day or two, they would all attend a play.

Chapter 7

Mary looked up toward the top of the warehouse as she climbed out of the carriage. The expression of awe she wore made Gabe smile.

"I have never been so close to the ships and buildings," she said as she took his hand so that he could help her from the carriage. "I have seen them in paintings and heard tell of gunboats, but I never imagined them to be so very large."

"They do not appear very big in paintings," Gabe agreed. "We will go through this door." He motioned to a door at the far end of the building and then extended an arm to both Miss Crawford and Mrs. Grant. "This door is not used by the dockhands. Just merchants and fellow owners such as myself. The whole building is not mine. There is a group of us, just as there is when we sponsor a privateer."

"Many hands make light work," Margaret said cheerily.

Gabe chuckled. Many hands also insured that one's

money did not have to be placed all in one venture and, therefore, kept the risk to himself at a manageable level.

He held the door open for Mary and her sister to enter ahead of him. The familiar smell of dust, wood, and men greeted him. He watched as Mary's nose crinkled at the first assault of the odor. It twitched adorably, but then, she smiled. She did not reach for her handkerchief to cover her nose as her sister did. She was made of less delicate things than some women. He liked that.

"The atmosphere takes a bit of getting used to." She leaned into his arm so that he could hear her over the noises of cargo being shifted, sorted, and stored. "I do not like rats," she added a little softer and with a sheepish grin.

"They are not a favourite of mine either," he replied. "Although, one must expect to deal with a few when in a warehouse or on a ship. It is just the nature of the work."

He led them up a set of stairs that went up to the second floor where his office was part of a row of rooms. Each belonged to one of his associates, and at the end of the row, there was a meeting room. That was where they gathered to argue about their next venture.

"This is where I spend a good deal of my time." He placed his hat on a hook.

"You can see everything from here." Mary stood at the window that faced the interior of the warehouse.

"And it is quieter," Margaret added. "I cannot imagine being able to do any proper thinking in that din out there."

Gabe chuckled. "It becomes familiar."

"What is in those casks?" Mary asked.

Some men were rolling a large barrel down the center of the warehouse.

"Rum," Gabe replied. "And that cart has spices. They are stored on the second floor. That hoist will see them to their place. And that crate is being lowered to a waiting wagon for some merchant. It is likely filled with a variety of items."

"It is all the world in one building."

"Very nearly." Gabe could not help but smile at Mary's wonder at all she was seeing. "Do you prefer the boats or the warehouse?" He turned toward his desk.

"I cannot say," Mary replied. "They are both of great interest. However, if I had to choose one..."

She had turned to look at him and was leaning against the window frame. Her lips pursed as she thought. He had never looked out toward the warehouse from his desk and seen such a lovely site as she made.

"I would choose the warehouse."

"What reasons do you have for your choice?"

She smiled. "That desk suits you."

"How so?"

She shrugged and crossed to stand in front of him with the well-suited desk between them. Her finger ran lightly over the surface, causing Gabe to swallow as he watched it. It was such a light, craveable touch.

"It is a trifle imposing, unlikely to be carted off by less than three strong men, and I dare say you could place one of those large casks on the top of it and the floor would give way before this desk crumbled." She looked up at him and smiled. "In other words, it seems rather trustworthy and honorable, much like the man standing behind it."

Gabe stood for a full minute with not a thing to say. He could not remember the last time he had been rendered speechless by anyone. While he may not have been able to speak, his mouth had no trouble smiling in what felt like a foolish fashion.

It was not as if he had never been praised before. He had. Many times. Some of those times had even been by a lady. However, there was something about hearing her, a lady who had very little reason to trust any man, calling him trustworthy and honorable that superseded any other moment of praise.

"I am flattered," he managed to say at last.

Her smile grew. "I like that about you."

"What precisely do you like?" She was causing his ability to reason to falter.

"You answer me honestly. Many men would have replied to such a description with some witty rejoinder or told me that a desk would most certainly not hold strong when a floor, which is built as solidly as this one is, would collapse. You have not once today spoken to me as a silly female."

"Because you are not." He was beginning to wish the sturdy desk would drop through the floor instead of standing between him and her — and it could take her sister with it. He would like nothing better than to be alone with her in this room right now.

"I would pick this warehouse because it is here and always will be," she said returning to the original topic of discussion. "It will not shift and float away on a current." She drew and released a breath. "And while it does have its rats and dust and aromas, it is tidy and well-organized. I like that." Her eyes sparkled. "And it does not creak like a boat does as it bobs up and down beside the quay."

He wondered if she was only speaking of his warehouse or if she were once again speaking of what she found appealing in a man. He could well imagine she would prefer a gentleman to be steady and unchanging. The admiral had been more like the ships he commanded – always prowling, looking for his next conquest.

"Durward." The door to his office swung open and one of his partners, Mr. Radcliff walked in. "I was on my way to my office and saw that we have visitors."

Radcliff was always curious to meet anyone new who entered the building. Some would call him friendly, but to Gabe, there was something about the way in which he did it that smacked more of a busybody.

"Allow me to introduce you to Miss Crawford and her sister Mrs. Grant."

"Ladies," Radcliff made a sweeping bow.

"This is Mr. Radcliff," Gabe continued. "He is a recent addition to our group."

"How recent?" Margaret asked.

"What has it been now? Six months?" Gabe asked Radcliff.

"Seven, Friday next," Radcliff replied. "I hear there is a meeting tomorrow. Is that correct?"

Gabe nodded. "There is a letter of marque to be discussed."

Radcliffe turned toward Mary and Margaret. "I hope you have not found your visit with us too taxing or tiresome."

"Oh, quite the contrary!" Margaret replied with some force. "This place is very stimulating. Is it not, Mary?"

"Excessively," Mary agreed. "I have never seen anything like this, so to me, it is fascinating."

"Well, Durward, I commend you on finding *friends...*" There was a lift to the word that made it more of a question than a statement. "...who are interested in what we do."

"Very fortunate," Gabe replied with a smile for Mary. He would let Radcliff wonder a bit longer about their relationship. He sat in his chair and unlocked the door on the right side of his desk. There was a ledger that he wished to take home. He had noticed a few numbers seemed to be off in the book in which he had been working last night, and he wanted to clarify any errors before tomorrow's meeting.

"My *cousin*..." Again, there was that questioning lift. This time it was accompanied by a questioning look at Gabe. "...is unwilling to even drive past the docks. This is why I think it is so unusual to meet two ladies who are not only willing to drive past but also stop and enter a warehouse."

"These things are not for every lady," Margaret assured him. "But I must admit to being a very curious sort of person, and when Mr. Durward suggested a tour, I could not resist. Mary is quite the same. Very curious."

Gabe frowned at the contents of his desk. He was certain he had placed the small black receipt book on top of the brown ledger and not the other way around as they were now. He shook his head. Perhaps he had not. It was not as if books could rearrange themselves. He took both books from the cupboard and put them on his desk. It would not hurt to give both books a thorough going over. In fact, the receipt book might prove handy in checking some of the figures in the other ledgers.

"Did you wish to stay longer to watch the workers?" he asked Mary.

She shook her head. "If you have what you need, I am content to leave."

He tucked the books into a leather satchel and took his hat from the wall.

"It has been lovely to meet you," Mary said to Radcliff before accepting Gabe's proffered arm.

"Likewise, likewise," Radcliff replied as he held the door open for them, his eyes were still filled with curiosity.

Gabe waited for Radcliff to move away from the door so that he could lock it. Then, he once again offered his arm to Mary and gave a nod of farewell to Radcliff. "There might be time for a short drive before I return you home if you are willing to spend a few more minutes with me."

"I am in no hurry to go home," Mary replied. "I do not know when I have enjoyed myself so much as today. I am certain none of my other suitors ever took me anywhere as interesting as this."

"It is because it is novel," Gabe returned. "I am certain that the first time you visited the museum, it was much more interesting than this warehouse and a few ships."

The laugh that answered such a comment was a sound Gabe would like to hear often.

"Again, you have answered me plainly instead of attempting to inflate the status of your business. However, there was one thing that the museum lacks compared to here."

"And what is that?" he asked as they descended the stairs.

"People," she replied.

"There are always people at the museum," he countered.

"But they are not part of the exhibit as it were," she

argued. "Today, I have gotten a glimpse, small as it might be, of another way of life. However, if you should like, you may take me to the museum, and then, I shall be able to tell you for certain which I find most interesting. For," she looked away, and a faint blush crept up her cheeks, "it might just be the company I am keeping which makes this warehouse so delightful."

"I am flattered," he replied quietly. "I must say that I have not found my warehouse as inviting as it was today while you and Mrs. Grant were here." He held her gaze for a moment before opening the door, so they could exit. She did not look away but met his eyes and smiled, and he noted there was barely a trace of wariness in her expression. And that, more than the pleasure she expressed in seeing his business or the flattering words she had bestowed upon him, buoyed his heart, for if she could trust him, she might just come to love him. His lips curled into a lopsided grin as he handed her into the carriage. His mother was right, it took very little for one's heart to decide its course.

Chapter 8

"You look lovely," Gabe whispered as he and Mary approached the theatre's entrance. "All will be well."

He had been telling her that for the past two days – ever since Henry's invitation to join him at the theatre had arrived during one of Gabe's daily calls on Mary. The calls were not all made during regular calling hours. Gabe's schedule did not always afford such luxuries, but Mary was happy to see him at any time of the day. Today, she had not seen him until now, and she had missed having him sit in the chair near the hearth, telling her about his day and inquiring after hers.

"Did you get the lace you needed?" he asked as they entered the building.

"No, Margaret and I were otherwise occupied today with a bit of knitting that the cat unravelled. We will get it tomorrow."

"I will be unable to call tomorrow. There is still a matter to argue about concerning the new letter of marque, and then I am engaged with another matter after that." He pulled her closer to his side as they reached the top of the stairs leading to the saloon where the private boxes were. "I will miss you."

Mary could not help smiling and blushing at his words. He knew her for all her faults, and yet, he liked her. He did not want anything from her in return – no connections, no introductions, no forced flirting or smiles. In fact, she was quite certain if she attempted a false smile, he would frown.

"I will miss you as well," she admitted so quietly that he had to tip his head towards her to hear it. She was finding herself very attached to him. It was becoming more and more difficult to keep the wall around her heart neatly intact.

"Here we are." He allowed her to enter the box ahead of him. "Mr. Crawford," he said with a smart nod of his head.

Henry returned the greeting and immediately set about making introductions. It was a small gathering of Henry's intended, Constance Linton; his friend, Charles Edwards; and Charles's fiancé, Evelyn Barrett.

"My brother could not be bothered to join us," Constance said as she settled into a chair. "And my aunt is keeping Mrs. Barret company."

"So that we can be rid of her for an evening," Evelyn added with a smile.

Charles smiled. "I shall find the lack of glaring to be refreshing."

Evelyn shook her head and laughed. "Mother no longer glares at you. She watches carefully, but she does not glare."

He shrugged. "I really do not mind either a careful observation or a glare as she can do nothing to prevent us from marrying. The papers have been signed and sent from my solicitor to your father's solicitor."

"Charles is only partially reformed," Henry whispered.

"I am not!" Charles cried. "I have left my dissipate ways behind, but I reserve the right to behave rakishly with my soon-to-be wife." He placed an arm around Evelyn's shoulders, which she swatted away.

"And this is why my mother watches closely," she said, leaning toward Mary. "But that is enough about us. We know very little about either of you."

Mary's cheeks burned. "I believe you know enough about me." Gabe took her hand. "I must apologize for the grief I had a part in creating for all of you." She blinked rapidly. Those blasted tears were far too ready to fall, and they mustn't.

"Miss Crawford is not who she was," Gabe added. "She is something far better."

Mary's smile wavered.

Charles's brow rose. "Time will be the proof of that, I suppose."

Gabe shook his head. "No, she is something far better than her old scheming self now, and with time, she shall only grow better and better." He tipped his head. "You are the fellow doing charity work, are you not?"

Charles nodded. "I have been working with some boys at Mrs. Verity's and helping feed the hungry."

"And informing me if he hears of anyone who is in need of a valet or footman or the like," Evelyn added.

"How long have you been doing this?"

Charles shrugged and looked at Evelyn. "A few weeks."

"That is not very long," Gabe replied with a grin, "but I suppose time will prove if this interest is a lasting thing or a passing fancy, is that not right?"

Charles shook his head and laughed. "I see your point. I have very little upon which to build my argument."

"Indeed," Gabe replied. "Miss Crawford is not very many days into her new journey, but I, for one, expect it will be a successful one. She is a most determined sort of lady."

Henry chuckled. "I can vouchsafe for that."

"Henry says you are in trade, Mr. Durward," Constance inserted, smiling at Mary, who was feeling, and likely looking, rather unsettled by the turn of the conversation.

She was delighted to hear Gabe defend her so valiantly, but it was a strange feeling and seemed out of place here where she sat with those she had offended. She deserved Mr. Edwards's censure. Miss Linton's compassion was not what she deserved.

"She has a good heart," Henry whispered in his sister's

ear while Gabe told Evelyn about having a warehouse and ships. "She does not hold your actions against you."

"How can she not?" Mary asked in surprise.

Henry shrugged. "As her brother always says, 'A shepherd does not beat the lost lamb when it returns to him.'"

Mary's brows rose high at such an odd statement.

"Trefor enjoys speaking in metaphors," Henry explained. "Unusual metaphors. You were lost, much as I was." He smiled at her. "But we are lost no longer."

Mary returned his smile and looked at Gabe. "No, we are not."

She had found her place in this world next to a gentleman whom she could trust and who demonstrated his belief in and care for her without apology. Moreover, she had not had to do one thing to convince him that he should attach himself to her. She laughed to herself. Mr. Durward did not strike her as the sort of man that anyone ever easily convinced to do anything if he did not wish to do it.

"Miss Crawford has visited my establishment," Gabe said, holding Mary's eyes with his intense gaze.

"Did you?" Evelyn asked eagerly. "I have only seen Mr. Gardiner's warehouse and only once, and I admit I was not paying particular attention to the building." Her cheeks coloured.

"Gardiner?" Gabe repeated.

"Yes," Evelyn answered. "Mr. Edward Gardiner. He also

provides some assistance at Mrs. Verity's home for orphans."

"He is a fine fellow," Gabe said. "Runs a good business, he does."

"It does seem to be prosperous," Charles said.

"I can assure you it is," Gabe replied. "He and I have made a deal or two since I arrived in London. He has a very discerning taste. You say you were at his warehouse?"

"The night Evelyn accepted my offer," Charles replied, once again putting his arm around her shoulders.

This time, Mary noticed, Miss Barrett did not swat him away. Instead, she ducked her head and blushed.

"I was there helping him with a project to see people in need given a warm meal."

"He runs a charity out of his warehouse?" Gabe asked.

Charles nodded as the actors began to take their places.

"Come see me at some point," Gabe whispered. "I may be in a position to help you with that."

"Business at the theatre?" Mary teased. "What would Mr. Bertram say?"

Gabe smiled and winked at her. "One must strike the deal wherever it presents itself." Once again, he took her hand, and, leaning closer to her, whispered, "Do you mind?"

Mind him holding her hand? She thought not and gave his hand a squeeze as she shook her head. The warmth of his touch spread like a delicious wave through her body. It was a good thing she was familiar with this play for, with as distracting as his nearness was, she would otherwise be very confused as to whom Agatha Friburg, Fredrick, and Baron Wildenhaim were and how their lives were entangled.

~*~*~

"Shall we find some refreshment?" Gabe asked as the intermission began.

"I would like that," Mary answered.

"And the rest of you?" Gabe said to others.

"I would like to stretch my legs," Evelyn said.

"You do not wish to remain here with me while the others go?" Charles asked her with a teasing grin.

Apparently, Mary thought, Mr. Edwards had been honest about reserving his rakish ways for his betrothed.

"No," Evelyn said. "I would rather walk with my hand on your arm than remain sitting here."

"We could stand. Over there behind the curtain."

"No dark corners, Mr. Edwards. My mother would not approve."

"But would you?" he asked as he stood and secured her hand in the crook of his arm.

"That is not a proper thing to ask a lady."

"Would you?" he asked again as they reached the door to their box.

"I am not completely opposed to the thought of kissing you. However, you did promise Mother that you would behave, and you know she would be told if someone were to see us. I, for one, do not wish to endure that lecture. Therefore, you will not be drawing me into any dark corners this evening, Mr. Edwards."

The arguing over propriety by the pair in front of them continued for some distance down the saloon while Henry and Constance walked at a slow pace behind Gabe and Mary.

"Miss Crawford," a lady in a green dress called to her.

Mary groaned. She had no desire to speak with Miss Morton, but she put on a smile and turned toward the lady.

"I have not seen you in this age," Miss Morton cooed to Mary while allowing her eyes to roam over Gabe's figure, smiling with approval of what she saw.

Mary bristled at the forwardness of her acquaintance.

"Sarah said you had given up polite society to take up with some tradesman," Miss Morton said in a loud whisper. "I had thought you a fool to do so, but now, I can see why," she once again gave Gabe an appreciative sweeping look.

Mary felt Gabe's arm flex under her hand.

"I apologize, Miss Morton, but Lady St. James has not been completely accurate in her accounting."

"She has not?" Miss Morton's hand flew to her heart as her eyes grew wide.

"I am afraid she has not been, for, you see, I have not

taken up with anyone from trade or otherwise. I grew weary of the constant inconstancy of our lot of supposed friends. Therefore, when I was presented with the opportunity to forge new friendships, I took it." She smiled up at Gabe. "And it has been a wonderfully wise decision. You should try it."

"Try what?" Miss Morton's brow drew together. That Miss Morton had missed the point of the comment was not a shock to Mary. Miss Morton was not particularly astute.

"Finding new friends who treat you well," Mary replied.

Miss Morton's brow remained furrowed. "But our friends do treat us well. I am never without an invitation to one thing or another."

"Then I am pleased for you," Mary replied with a curtsey before Miss Morton could say more.

"She is not excessively intelligent, is she?" Gabe asked as they moved away from Miss Morton.

"She would likely stand outside and stare at a door instead of going through it if she was told it was only for going out and not coming in," Mary replied.

Gabe chuckled and then asked her what her preferred beverage was before going to procure it.

Other than Miss Morton, no other friend approached Mary, though many were there, and it was not because they did not see her. No, they made a point of looking directly at her and then turning away.

"That was not pleasant," Gabe said as they once again took their seats.

Mary had to agree. Being snubbed was not pleasant, but... "It was not as horrid as I thought it might be."

"It was not?"

She shook her head. "It is likely because you were standing with me."

"Then you have no regrets about leaving your former friends behind."

Again, she shook her head. "Very little. I do miss the calls and invitations to some degree. Sitting at home can be dull. Margaret hosts the occasional dinner for Dr. Grant's friends, but," she shrugged, "it is different."

His eyes were filled with concern.

"Do not worry," she said. "I am content. Truly I am."

To Mary, the remaining portion of the play was over far more quickly than she would have liked it to be. It had been a delight sitting close enough to Mr. Durward that their shoulders touched and he could discreetly hold her hand.

"You acquitted yourself very well this evening," Gabe said as he climbed into the carriage and took the seat across from her.

Mary shook her head and laughed lightly.

"Do you not believe me?" he asked, leaning toward her as the carriage began to move.

"It is not that," she mirrored his action and leaned toward him.

"Then what is it?" he asked.

"I do not think I shall ever get used to hearing someone speak of me as if they are proud of something I have done – something good that I have done," she clarified. "I like it."

"As you should," he replied in his normal pragmatic fashion. "Trust me, it will eventually become normal."

She smiled and looked at him for a long moment while a wonderfully frightening thought overtook her. She placed a hand on his where it lay on his knee. "I do trust you," she said, putting her thought into words.

His replying smile was worth enduring the nervous twisting of her stomach and fluttering of her heart that had accompanied admitting something like that to him.

"I shall guard that trust with my very life," he said, grasping her hand in his while placing his other hand on her cheek. "I will not play on it or with it as some might."

She leaned her cheek into his hand and closed her eyes. She knew the words he spoke were true. She did not know how she knew it, but she did. It was likely because he was so unwaveringly honest with her. He had not once flattered her. He had not once attempted to goad her into praising him. And he had always treated her as if she mattered – not for her beauty but for herself.

Her eyes fluttered open as she felt his lips touch the cheek that was not cupped in his hand. His eyes questioned hers, and with a smile of happiness that spread from her lips through her heart and down to her cold toes in her boots, she gave him the permission he sought to claim her lips in a kiss that was, at the same time, both a gentle caress and a firm pledge of his loyalty.

"I'll never let you take on water," he murmured before, capturing her face between his hand and kissing her more ardently.

Chapter 9

The day had been a long one, so Gabe was happy to see Tom darken the door to his office, signalling that it was nearly time to leave.

"Mrs. Grant wished for you to have this." Tom placed a small parcel on Gabe's desk. "It seems both she and Miss Crawford are excessively fond of you. Those are some tasty biscuits, and you did not even have to hold a ball of yarn for any length of time in order to be worthy of one." Tom dropped into a chair.

"You called on Mrs. Grant?" He smiled as he opened the parcel. It was, indeed, filled with five biscuits but that is not what made him smile.

"What is it?" Tom asked, leaning forward to look at the package on Gabe's desk.

"Biscuits," Gabe said. "Would you like one? I am certain I can find some wool or some such thing around here for you to hold to prove your worth."

Tom laughed. "The biscuit, I will take, but you may keep

your yarn." And he did claim a biscuit. "Now, what has you smiling like a smitten fool?"

"Miss Crawford," Gabe said as he settled back in his chair to enjoy his treat and the knowledge that Mary missed him. "She wrote a message on the paper."

Tom pulled the paper towards him and looked at it. "Your chair is empty? You have a chair at the Grants?"

Gabe nodded.

"Oh, how shall I explain to my brother that my friend has married Miss Crawford?" Tom asked as he flopped back in his chair.

"We are not betrothed," Gabe answered. "We are just very good friends."

"That smile says it is more."

Gabe shrugged. "Perhaps it is."

"Do you intend to offer for her?"

"Perhaps."

"Again, your smile says it is more than perhaps."

"Perhaps," Gabe replied once again. Oh, he intended to offer for Mary. He had known he would for several days now, but it was not until last night when she had admitted to him that she trusted him and allowed him to kiss her that he had determined he would make his offer sooner rather than later. One must secure the deal when the opportunity arose so that one did not lose out to another, did he not? He was confident that that was as true with ladies as it was with ships and cargo. Precious commodities were not something to risk losing, especially when it was a ruby such as Miss Crawford. She did look lovely in red.

"What is the sticking point?" Tom asked.

"She has yet to meet my mother." Gabe picked up a second biscuit from the packet in front of him. "What do you need, Radcliff?" He looked past Tom to the man standing in the doorway.

"I have come to tell you that it has been decided to take your suggestion and employ thirty-three rather than twenty-eight."

"I am glad that Perkins finally saw reason."

"You hold the greatest number of shares, and without those, the venture would be ill-advised."

Gabe nodded. "As I said, I am glad Perkins finally saw reason. The extra men will be needed once the prize is taken. Even if she is only towed to port, there must be crew on her."

Radcliff looked as if he wanted to say something but would not, which was not surprising as the man never seemed to truly speak his mind. He was always parroting someone else. It was a trait that Gabe found excessively annoying.

"The extra expense is insurance," Gabe replied. He was certain that the man was, like the others, concerned about the loss of revenue from the hiring of extra men. "My share is the largest, so the expense falls most heavily on me as does the loss."

"Of course, Durward. The others and I understand your position."

"Yet, you are not happy about it."

"A loss of funds is a loss of funds."

"It is, but you can rest easy knowing that I will feel it more than you."

"Of course, of course." He gave a nod to both Gabe and Tom and took his leave.

"I take it there was a debate about the size of the crew on your next venture."

Gabe nodded. "My last venture of this sort."

"Last?" Shock suffused Tom's tone.

Again, Gabe nodded. "I find I would rather invest my monies in something more secure."

"Such as?"

Gabe shrugged. "I have not entirely decided."

"And what is the reason for this shift?"

"Miss Crawford."

"But did you not say she was interested in your ships and warehouse?"

Gabe nodded. "There are men who have boats and buildings, but they do not also risk substantial amounts of their money in ventures that could see that money, as well as a boat and its crew, lost to them. Privateers are not always the victor. Sometimes they are the spoil."

"This is true, but will you be happy to put aside the thrill of the risk?"

That was a question Gabe had been pondering ever since Mary had stood in this office, but then last night as he attempted to sleep, he had come to the conclusion that he was once again standing on the beach of a tropical island. Only this time there was no hole in his arm, but a possible hole that would be left in his heart if he were to lose either Mary or her trust. "I am at peace."

Tom shook his head in bewilderment. "I never expected you to give this up."

"Wars are not always with us. Strife ebbs and flows, and the usefulness and profitability of a privateer is only as long as the conflict, my friend."

"True, true. You have a point. Do not tell me you are thinking of purchasing an estate?"

Gabe chuckled. "Then I will not tell you."

"What?" Tom cried. "I said it in jest."

"I have considered it as a future possibility. If I have children, it might be best for them. I have not made any decision regarding it, however, as I think that decision should be made by both the father and mother of said children."

"You are serious about offering for Miss Crawford, then?"

Gabe chuckled as Tom shook his head in wonder.

"After she has met my mother." His brows rose. "Mother can be an acquired taste. She is not backward in stating her opinions and expecting things to be done her way."

"Much like her son," Tom said with a laugh.

"Yes, I suppose you are correct there, although Father was also set in his ways."

"What has you poring over the accounts today? Regular concerns or was your frown before I entered something more than the debate about crew members?"

"You mean the debate from which I and my shares walked away?" Gabe asked with a grin.

Tom chuckled and shook his head.

"It was effective. Logic and reasoning had done little good in the last meeting and for the first half hour of today's meeting. But that was not the reason for my frown. Something is not adding up in my accounts. There should be a greater profit margin than there is. I cannot put my finger on it, but something is not right." He sighed. "And that is another reason to give this up. I wish to be my own man – completely. I do not wish to be part of a conglomerate of men. It seems little better than the company. The men I work with are good men to a point, but then there is greed that surfaces and safety and security must be pushed to the side to increase the amount of the take."

"And that is not how you prefer to operate."

It was not a question. Tom knew that, while Gabe enjoyed an adventure and the risk involved, he had his limits. Gabe wanted things to be done with integrity, for character was more important to him than gold. He had seen men make some deplorable decisions in an attempt to improve the company's position in India and their own within the company. Corruption and lack of concern for others was not something of which Gabe wished to ever be part.

"No, it is not, and as long as I must be beholden to some-one other than myself, I shall always face the prospect of being forced to concede to such things."

"Especially if someone were to put up more shares than you."

Gabe nodded and closed his books. "These will wait until tomorrow." He gathered them up and stacked them in the cabinet in his desk. Then, slipping the key in his pocket, he ate the last biscuit, folded Mary's note, and placed it in his pocket before standing and adding, "Mother cannot wait." He put on his hat and coat and fol-lowed Tom out of the office. "You are joining us, are you not?"

"I would not wish to run the risk of offending your mother before we have even met."

Gabe chuckled. "She will like you. I am certain of it."

They exited the building together and entered Tom's carriage. Gabe had taken a hack this morning as he knew Tom would be calling for him and coming to dinner.

"Have you made any progress in finding a wife?" Gabe asked as they settled in and the carriage began to move. He knew that that was the goal of Tom's participation in the season.

"Very little, but I am hopeful."

"I will do my best to alert you of any possibilities I find, but I am not out in society much these days, although I did attend the theatre last night with Miss Crawford and her brother."

Tom lifted the side curtain with the tip of his cane to look out. "What did you see?"

"Lovers' Vows."

"You saw what?" Tom's attention was fully on Gabe.

"Lovers' Vows. Do you know it?" Gabe grinned. He knew very well that Tom knew the play better than most as Mary had told him about the disastrous attempt to stage a performance at Mansfield Park.

Tom laughed. "I am intimately acquainted with it, as I am certain you know."

"Indeed, I do." Gabe leaned his head against the squabs. "I must say I have never enjoyed sitting in one place for so long before." Nor had he enjoyed a ride in a carriage as much as he had that ride last night when Mary had allowed him to kiss her several times.

They rode in silence for a distance until the carriage came to a stop, shaking Gabe from his pleasant reverie of carriages and kissing.

"Are we at your house already?" Tom asked, pushing the curtain aside with his cane once again.

"There seems to be a carriage that has had some trouble," Gabe said as he peered out the window. Being on the forward-facing seat, he could see what Tom could not. "I will see if I can be of service."

~*~*~

"Miss Morton," he greeted as he approached the carriage in front of them. The lady from last night at the theatre was standing to the side, watching, with two other young ladies whom he did not know.

"Oh, it is the most dreadful thing, Mr. Durward," she cried. "The wheel is broken. I do not know how this could happen. Father takes such good care of his vehicles."

Gabe was quite certain that the lady before him had very little idea about how a wheel could break or how one cared for a vehicle of any sort. Still, he smiled and offered his assistance. "Allow me to see if I can help the men. Another set of hands might make moving the carriage easier."

"But how shall we get home?"

"The carriage must be moved first," he said as calmly as he could.

"All those packages must be kept safe," said one of her friends. "I do not trust those strangers near them."

"No one is going to steal your parcels," Gabe assured them. Mary must have felt very out of place with some of her friends, for she was a great deal more astute and master of her emotions than these ladies appeared to be. "These men are just attempting to clear the road so others can get through the street."

"But they are tradesmen," the other of Miss Morton's friends said.

"As am I," Gabe said, levelling a firm stare in her direction. He despised rudeness. "Would you rather move the vehicle by yourselves?"

"You are a tradesman?" the lady asked in disbelief. "You do not look like one."

"We do not all wear smocks," he replied and made to move to where he could lend a shoulder to help get the vehicle out of the path so that he could go home.

"A very heroic deed, Mr. Durward," Lady St. James said as Gabe brushed dirt from his clothing after the road had been cleared and he was moving toward his carriage.

"Indeed, it was," Miss Morton said, stepping forward to offer him her hand in thanks.

He caught her by the elbow when she tripped. "It was not heroic," he said with a look toward Lady St. James as he steadied Miss Morton. "I would like to eat dinner before it is cold, and Miss Morton's vehicle was in the way of our vehicle. It was an act of necessity." He extracted his arm which had become ensnared in Miss Morton's grasp. "If you will excuse me, Mr. Bertram is waiting, and as I said, we do not wish to be late for dinner."

"And we must see that our parcels are delivered home safely," Lady St. James replied. "Shopping can be so taxing. Come along, ladies. My coach has ample room for both you and your things."

Gabe wished them well with a tip of his hat and then brushed at a few remaining patches of dust and returned to Tom's carriage, so he could be on his way home.

Chapter 10

Mary looked over the selection of lace that was presented to her. The first was too large. The second was a bit too delicate, as was the third. But the fourth, the fourth looked like it would suit her project quite well.

"A fine selection, do you not think, Emily?" Lady St. James picked up the lace from the counter with a glance at one of her three companions. "Not too delicate. Very serviceable. Quite fitting for a trades man's wife."

"Oh, this is not for a lady. This is for a blanket for a wee one," Margaret inserted before Mary could say anything.

"It is not for yourself then?" Lady St. James directed the question to Mary, making clear to Margaret the implication of her former statement, as she handed the lace to Miss Morton.

"Oh, no," Margaret cried. "Have no fear. Mary shall have better lace than that when she finally weds. I shall see to that. But it is kind of you to be concerned."

Mary sucked in on her cheeks to keep from smiling at how Margaret feigned ignorance of Sarah's disparagement rankled Sarah. Margaret had always been very good at that. She did not like confrontations, and so she often tried to turn them away by presenting the aggressor with the frustrating task of attempting to make her display any sort of anger. Mary knew she would hear a full litany of rebukes of Lady St. James on their way home, but Margaret would not stoop to saying such things in public.

"It is very serviceable," Emily Morton said as she handed the lace to Margaret.

"I am glad you think so," Mary said. "A child's blanket should always be serviceable. A bit of this on it will just make it a little bit more special."

"A child?" There was laughter in Lady St. James's voice. "Whose child?" She looked toward Miss Morton, Miss Smith, and Miss Wilson as she covered her mouth with the tips of her fingers. "Mr. Durward is a handsome fellow." The three ladies with her tittered.

"He is, but he has no children," Margaret once again intervened. "This is for the poor souls at the foundling hospital."

"Are you certain he has none?" Lady St. James said, her eyes flashing with wicked delight.

"Quite," Margaret assured her. "He is not the sort."

Lady St. James lowered her voice. "I understand the seafaring sort are most proficient at leaving their unwanted offspring in foreign ports, so I am sure you are correct. None of the children in one of *our* hospitals would be *his*."

"No, you misunderstand me," Margaret said in a flat tone that told Mary her sister was reaching the end of her patience. "I meant he is an honourable gentleman."

"My lady knows very little about those sorts of gentlemen," Mary said. "So, you will have to forgive her ignorance in such things, Margaret."

"I know very well of what I speak," Sarah snapped. "We just saw your Mr. Durward. Miss Morton's carriage was unfortunate enough to sustain a broken wheel, and since it was in the middle of the road, it was preventing traffic from moving freely. Mr. Durward assisted in the removal of the vehicle to the side of the road." She sighed. "He is a magnificent specimen."

"That only proves his character as good," Margaret said when Sarah paused.

"I will take this one," Mary said, turning to the clerk, who assured her it would be wrapped up straightaway.

"I have not finished," Sarah said. "What was the name of the lady he was on his way to visit?" She turned toward her friends. "I am dreadful at remembering such details when things are so chaotic as they were with the traffic not moving and the tradesmen pushing that carriage out of the way. It really was quite the sight."

"I do not remember," Miss Morton said. "Do you?" She turned to the other ladies, who assured her they did not remember either.

"Oh, wait!" Miss Smith cried. "Was it Isla?"

Lady St. James considered the name and then shook her head. "I am not certain it was, but it was, of course, an exotic sounding name. Men who have sailed the seas do prefer their mistresses to be foreign. She must be rather special as he seemed in quite the hurry to be on his way." She placed a hand on Mary's arm. "It is shocking, I suppose, to tell you this. However, Mr. Bertram was with him, so I suppose whoever this mistress is resides with other ladies of her trade."

Mary's brow furrowed. Mr. Durward was not visiting a brothel accompanied by Mr. Bertram. Tom had said he intended to be a proper gentleman from this point forward. He had not sounded like a man who was unsure of his decision when he had spoken to her that night in the garden. And Gabe? She was nearly certain he was not the sort of gentleman who would take a mistress after the way he has spoken so harshly about the admiral.

However, "You must be mistaken," was all she could think to say to Sarah.

"We all think that the first time our gentlemen are discovered to be amusing themselves without us." She shrugged. "But it is the way things are."

"No, it is not. Not for everyone," Mary countered. Edmund would have never taken a mistress, and if one gentleman would not, then, surely, there were others who were just as trustworthy.

Sarah patted Mary's arm and smiled at her sadly. "We all

start out denying it is possible, but when you have discovered the truth of my words, send me word, and I shall have an invitation for you to our next soiree." She grimaced. "However, I cannot include you while you are still courting Mr. Durward. My husband would just not approve. I am certain you understand. It is not that I do not wish to have you join us, but my husband is the holder of the purse, after all."

Mary smiled and nodded before saying a word of farewell. Her eyes narrowed as she walked out of the store with her parcel. "It is not true!"

"Of course, it is not true," Margaret assured her. "You, of all people, should know how proficient Lady St. James is at crafting a tale."

Mary nodded. She knew that Sarah was not to be trusted. She also knew that Mr. Durward was trustworthy. However, the fear of being proven wrong about him and having her heart shatter would not be easily tucked away. She drew in a breath through her nose and slowly blew it out through slightly parted lips. She did this three times, and yet the racing of her heart and the threat of tears did not diminish.

"Come. We will take a drive before we go home," Margaret suggested.

Mary shook her head. She did not wish to be trapped in a carriage with her sister when she would rather be in her room where no one would know if she gave in to those tears that wished so desperately to be set free. However, since Margaret would not be put off, they drove in some direction that was not the way home.

They had turned down a second street before anything was said in the carriage. Margaret sat next to Mary and held her hand but said nothing. It always amazed Mary how Margaret knew the right thing to do. It was a quality that made Margaret an excellent older sister as well as a welcoming parson's wife. Again, Mary was reminded of how ill-suited she was to Edmund. She would not have been a good parson's wife.

"Tears are not evil," Margaret whispered. "If you need to cry, you may. I will not tell anyone."

Mary shook her head.

"Why do you fear them?" Margaret asked.

Mary drew and expelled a breath, attempting to steady herself, before replying. "Tears are a sign of weakness. A lady who cries acknowledges her hurt and others can use that against her." She rested her head back and closed her eyes. "The admiral seemed to enjoy seeing his wife in tears, and she attempted to use them to sway him but with no success." She opened her eyes and looked at Margaret. "Nothing good comes from tears that are shed in public."

"We are not in public, and I would not rejoice in your pain. Surely, you know that!"

Mary squeezed the hand that held hers. "I do, but I fear that if I succumb to tears once, even in this carriage with only you as my audience, I shall do so again." She shrugged. "I know it does not make sense, but it just does not feel safe to allow myself to cry unless I am in private."

Margaret shook her head and scowled. "I could box the admiral's ears! Oh, he is heinous! To think he has caused you to be so! It is as if he controls you even now."

Mary gasped. Would she ever be rid of that man? Crying put her at risk of being humiliated and laughed at, but by not shedding a tear, she was still living in the admiral's shadow.

"What is it?" Margaret asked in concern. "I did not mean to startle you with my outcry, but he makes me so angry."

Mary understood that feeling. The admiral had been making her angry for years. "It was the truth of what you said that startled me. Please, do not think you have wounded me."

"If you are certain you are well," Margaret replied hesitantly.

With a nod, Mary assured her sister that she was as well as could be expected.

"Then, shall we go home?"

"I think we should," Mary said.

Margaret tapped the wall behind the driver, and after the carriage had stopped and a footman had inquired as to what was needed, they began their homeward journey.

"I am positive," Margaret said, looking out the window,

"that I do not even know where we are. These buildings do not look at all familiar." She turned to Mary. "We should do this more often."

"Do what more often?" Mary leaned toward the window to look up at the tops of the houses and down the street. They stood row on row next to each other with their tops nearly identical in height.

"Wander about and discover more of town. We have been here for some time now, and there is yet so much to see."

"I would like that."

"It will be an adventure much like it was that day we visited Mr. Durward at his warehouse." Margaret's breath tickled Mary's ear as she leaned close to join Mary in looking out the window. "I think it is excellent to understand how different people live. Very much like visiting the foundling hospital, visiting new neighbourhoods will give us an appreciation for all we have." She sat back, though she still leaned toward Mary and peered out the window. "Of course, our driver will know if it is a neighbourhood we should visit. I should not want to see you in any danger. That simply would not do."

"I would not wish to be in danger," Mary assured her. "I am curious to a point, but it is not to the point of risking my safety. When it comes to such things, I would prefer to be told about the state of things by someone else who has survived the dangers."

They turned once again, causing Margaret to slide a little bit closer to Mary.

Mary's breath caught in her chest, and her hand covered her heart.

"Margaret," she whispered, unable to make any louder sound. "It is Mr. Durward and Mr. Bertram." A tear slid down her cheek. "He was..." she attempted, as her sister peered out the window, to tell her that she had seen Mr. Durward allowing the woman at the door to kiss him, but words failed her.

"Oh, I see him!" Margaret cried. "Who is that?"

Mary shook her head. Hopefully, it was not the mistress Sarah had mentioned. Tom entered the house first, then, the exotic-looking woman, who had welcomed Mr. Durward with a kiss, wrapped her arms around one of his arms, and happily, he entered with her as a second, third, and fourth tear slid down Mary's cheek.

Chapter 11

"It seems," Tom said the next day as he once again found himself settling into a chair in front of Gabe's desk at the warehouse, "that Lady St. James had a brooch go missing yesterday when she was out shopping." He placed a copy of the newspaper on Gabe's desk.

Gabe nodded. "I read that. Some light-fingered pickpocket snatched it." He shook his head. "A pretty young lady with an ability to trip over nothing into the arms of a gentleman is more like it!"

"In any case," Tom replied, "you were right in turning it into the fellows at Bow Street as soon as you discovered it in your pocket, even if it did make us late for dinner."

"It is always best to deal with the nefarious before they can spin their web too wide. Unless, of course, you cannot find the nefarious creature." He pushed his books forward.

"Are you still missing money?"

Gabe nodded. He had explained to Tom last night how he had noticed about a month ago that the accounts were not adding up as they should – as they always had in the past.

"And your partners? Have you spoken to them?"

Again, Gabe nodded. "They are going to scour the books starting tomorrow. I have one last day to discover my error, or it is going to look very much like I have made the money go missing."

"But you are the one who reported it! A thief does not point out his pilfering."

If only that was what all of his partners believed, but from the whispers he had heard since telling them of the discrepancy this morning, they did not. He blew out a breath. "Well, if that report had kept my name out of it as the person who found and returned the brooch, perhaps everyone would believe as you do."

"You cannot be serious!" Tom cried.

"But I am. I have heard a few snatches of conversations that lead me to believe there are those who think I am only reporting the missing funds because I am afraid I will get caught – just as I returned that brooch once I knew that Lady St. James had noticed it was missing."

"But you had no way of knowing that Lady St. James was going to report the brooch as stolen! You did not even know it was hers, and you turned it in at Bow Street before she even made her report."

"I know that, but you know how things can be twisted by those who are not fond of you."

Tom reluctantly agreed. Both he and Gabe knew that there were many in society who twisted and turned information for their purpose.

"My position in the business is tenuous at present," Gabe admitted. "I planned to make my break from my partners soon, but I had hoped to claim one more prize before doing so. I can sustain the blow if I am asked to depart, but it will not be as easily done as if I left on my own terms and without having to repay the money that is missing." He sucked in another breath. Being dismissed and having to repay funds was the best option. "Of course, if they decide to pull me into Old Bailey's, the outcome would be even worse, which is why I have asked you to join me today."

He rose and closed the door. He did not need to have anyone who happened to pass by hearing what he had to say, and he could hear distant footsteps in the corridor.

"I have created a list of items that will need someone to look after them if I cannot. There is information here and instructions regarding my finances, but the most important are the last two items." He handed the list to Tom. "I know it is a lot to ask, but if you could in some way see that Mother is settled into a comfortable place. Father left her ample money to do so." He swallowed against the emotions that saying such a thing necessarily roused in him. "And then, there is the matter of that ring I showed you last night. I wish for Miss Crawford to have it no matter what becomes of me. I want her to know that I truly did care for her." He shook his head. "You will have to convince her that I did not steal anything, or she will likely not take the ring as she has no desire to be reminded of yet another untrustworthy gentleman."

He scrubbed his face. In all of this, he worried the most about Mary. She had just come to trust him. If these lies were to be spread widely and reach her, that fledgling trust would be destroyed and most likely irreparably. He shook his head, unwilling to contemplate it further.

Tom looked over the list before folding it and putting it in his pocket while assuring Gabe that he would see everything was done that was necessary. "But I cannot see it being a necessity. A repayment of funds, I can see, but you have worked with these men for three years now! They must know how concerned you are about seeing things done correctly."

"They are also put out with me after our difference of opinion on the number of crew members to send on the next voyage."

"But to the point of consigning your life away?" Tom gave him a look of utter disbelief.

"I just want to be prepared for all eventualities, and we have taken on three new partners in the last year. None of them have put up as much money as I have, but they seem eager to challenge me for the position."

"Have any of them had access to these ledgers?"

Gabe shook his head. "I was appointed the overseer of the accounts three months ago."

The two good friends fell into pensive silence. Gabe was certain that Tom was attempting to reason out what could have happened, just as he was. He wished him luck, for he had been pondering it for three weeks now – since the first appearance of a discrepancy between what was reported in the coffers and in his ledger.

Gabe sighed, breaking the silence. "I should just bring them the missing funds and be done with it and them. They can keep the accounts. They can fit the boat for the next journey without my funds or input. I should just wash my hands of the whole business."

"But?"

"I cannot. I did not lose or steal that money, and I shall not pay for the sins of another until I am forced to do so."

Tom rose as Gabe closed his ledger and slipped it into his leather satchel.

"Are you calling at the Grants' home?" Tom asked.

"I would like to."

"Do you mind if I join you?"

Gabe shook his head. "I find I wish to be surrounded by friends at the moment."

Tom clapped him on the shoulder. "All will work out for the best, my friend."

"I wish I had your well of optimism." He stopped to look out over the floors of the warehouse. How he enjoyed all of this activity and the excitement of the arrival of new goods! He would miss this.

"Mr. Durward!"

Gabe turned toward one of the things about this place he would not miss. "How may I be of service, Mr. Radcliff?" The man was an ever-present, bothersome shadow.

"We did not want to miss you before you left," he held out a missive to Gabe. "I am to tell you that someone will pick up the books from your home tomorrow. There is no need for you to come in until things are resolved."

So they were going to oust him before they even examined the evidence? How noble!

"I have orders to be filled," Gabe said.

"Someone will see to them. It is all there in the note."

Gabe scanned the note. "Well, then, seeing as you require my key, allow me to gather my personal effects before you lock me out of my office – an office for which I have paid on time as required for several years."

Radcliff scampered after him as Gabe returned to his office with long determined strides to collect the few items which were his and place them in a small crate that was normally used for collecting paper to be burned. Outrage at this sort of high-handed treatment overspread him.

"You do not mind if I use this crate, do you?" He skewered Radcliff with a harsh glare. "As you can see I am not taking anything that is not solely and completely mine aside from this crate, which I will return with the ledgers in the morning."

"I am certain that is acceptable," Radcliff replied.

Gabe thrust his key into the weaselly fellow's hand and barely refrained from giving in to the wish to slam the door. However, there was no need to draw undue notice.

"He seemed happy to see you go," Tom commented as they exited the building.

"We have never gotten on well," Gabe explained. "He is too fond of simpering."

Tom chuckled. "Yes, I can see how that would annoy a fellow like yourself."

"It should annoy anyone with sense," Gabe retorted. "Tossed out of my own office before one of them has even taken a look at the blasted books! I told you, Tom, they are not a sensible lot. It is why I have given you that list. It might very well become necessary."

"It is a precaution. Both your list and their actions." Tom settled into his carriage across from Gabe whose horse was being ridden by a groom behind them. "They do not want you to have an opportunity to magically make the money reappear or more to disappear. Not that you would or have or anything like that."

Gabe huffed. Years of working with a group of men and this was the trust they gave him! It was truly no better than the company. It, like the company, was a corrupted entity. It was just smaller in scale, but no matter how large a business might be, there was always the danger of someone acting with little integrity and a lot of greed.

"It is what you would do," Tom ventured, earning himself a glare from Gabe.

"Most likely." He did not want to admit it, but it was more than likely how he would handle a situation where someone was suspected of theft.

"In a way," Tom continued. "It protects you. If something were to go missing tonight, you could not be held responsible."

"Nothing will go missing tonight," Gabe grumbled. Whoever was behind the missing money did not seem stupid enough to make himself so obvious. Until this moment, Gabe had not considered very seriously that someone was doing more than making him look bad to undermine his position in the partnership.

"How can you be so certain?" Tom asked.

"I am not, but it seems that if there is someone in that place who wishes me gone, they will not do something to help prove my innocence."

It was the only explanation that made sense to him. Very much like Lady St. James and her helpful friend Miss Morton who had attempted to make him look guilty yesterday, whoever was swindling his business was attempting to take him down in the process.

In the case of Lady St. James, Gabe knew what she held against him. However, in regard to his business, he did not know the motivation behind the actions taken since just wishing to be lead shareholder did not seem to be a strong enough reason.

Tom allowed it to be true and turned the discussion somewhat. "Do you still wish to call on Miss Crawford?"

Gabe closed his eyes and tipped his head back against the squabs. He longed to see Mary. Since yesterday, after speaking to Tom about the missing funds and agreeing with him that it was wisest to inform his partners sooner rather than later of the incongruities in the accounts, he had longed to see Mary and tell her of his troubles. Whether or not she would willingly help him bear such difficulties, he was not sure, but just the thought of having her beside him as he dealt with this mess had comforted him enough to find a few hours of sleep.

Now, he longed to see her so that he might have one last opportunity to convince her of his integrity and see her beautiful face just one more time – if it should, indeed, happen to be the last. He heaved a sigh.

"I should say my farewells, I suppose. Just in case." He had a dreadful feeling that things were going to get worse before they got better – if they ever got better.

"I would suggest a pint before we call. It seems you could use something to help lift your morose mood. It is unlike you."

To Gabe, it seemed a good idea. If things went poorly, as they seemed to be doing, he was in danger of losing something of far greater value than his business. His heart would be utterly crushed if Mary were to turn him away or if he had to walk away from her, and that knowledge, more than any of his other present trials, was the root of his morose. Therefore, he needed a few minutes to collect himself before he presented himself to Miss Crawford. And so, they stopped for a pint before arriving at the Grants.

~*~*~

"Henry?" Tom said as he exited the carriage before Gabe. "What has you pacing in front of Dr. Grant's house?"

"Dr. Grant is about to have an apoplexy, and I cannot sit still and watch that." Henry shook his head, turned away from them, and looked up the street.

"I am not certain I understand your meaning," Gabe said. "Are you waiting for the physician to arrive?"

Again, Henry shook his head and with a wave of his hand toward the house added, "The physician is in there."

"You mean to say, Dr. Grant is truly ill?" Tom asked.

Henry removed his hat and ran a hand through his hair. "Not without reason." He looked at Gabe. "Did my sisters come to see you today?"

Gabe shook his head. "I have not seen either of your sisters in two days."

"Well, as upset as Mary was with you, I did not expect they would have, but I had to ask."

Gabe glanced at Tom who looked just as confused as Gabe felt. Mr. Crawford had always struck Gabe as a fellow that was in good control of his faculties, but at present, the man seemed to be nearly wild with illogicalness.

"Henry," Tom said quietly, "why was Mary upset with Gabe?"

"Some woman," Henry paced away from them and back. "What am I to do? They should have been home an hour ago? Mary will sometimes run late to her time, for she says she cannot be dictated to by a watch, but Margaret? Margaret is as constant as the sun's rising. She is always punctual to her time."

"It would help us greatly if you would tell us all the bits and pieces about what you are speaking," Gabe suggested.

"Maybe while consuming some port," Tom offered.

"Bow Street!" Henry cried. "I could go to Bow Street. They are good at finding people."

Panic was beginning to build within Gabe. "Tell me what has happened?" he demanded, taking Henry by the shoulders before the man could fly off to Bow Street.

"I do not know what has happened," Henry replied. "I attempted to see Mary last evening, but she was not up to seeing anyone. In fact, she was as beside herself as I have ever seen her."

"And why was that?"

"Because you were being greeted by some exotic mistress."

"I beg your pardon?" Gabe nearly shouted. "I have no mistress."

"I do not believe you do!" Henry shouted back. "But, my sisters saw you being greeted with a kiss at some house somewhere, although they did not know where they were. She and Margaret had gone for a drive after Lady St. James had been vicious upon meeting them at a store and put the notion of your having a mistress in Mary's head, which is why I do not believe they saw what they thought they saw. Lady St. James is not known for refraining from concocting stories that suit her purposes."

Gabe shook his head. Lady St. James had been working long and hard yesterday to do her damage it seemed. That is was his mother Mary had seen could be explained later. For now, he only wished to know why Henry seemed so frantic. So, he remained quiet and allowed Henry to continue.

"Mary and Margaret went for a walk in the park today and were supposed to be home to receive me an hour ago. They have yet to appear, and just before the physician was summoned, we received word that they had not returned to their carriage nor could they be seen in the portion of the park where they said they would be."

"They are missing?" Panic bloomed in all its glory within Gabe. His heart, though it was beating at a ferocious pace, seemed to have fallen into his stomach, causing him to feel both nauseous and lightheaded.

Henry nodded. "And I have no idea where to look to find them."

Gabe turned and looked up and then down the street, hoping that by some miracle, Henry could be wrong, and Mary would be seen returning home. But she was not. He must keep his wits about him. He knew he must. It was the only way to survive a skirmish. What they needed was a plan.

Turning back to Henry and Tom, he said, "I must take those ledgers home so that they are there when the messenger calls for them tomorrow, and then..." He was at a loss for how to continue. He knew how to track the enemy on the sea, but on land and when the enemy was not known to him? He could not formulate a plan. He only knew that he must, simply must, find Mary.

Chapter 12

The sound of lapping water and the rocking motion of whatever hard object Mary sat against stirred her. She groaned as she attempted to turn her head. Her eyes flew open when she found she could not lift her hand to rub the sore spot on her head. Her hands and feet were tied, and the rope around them was connected in such a way that she could not straighten her legs without leaning forward. Nor could she lift her hands without tugging her feet towards herself. Someone leaned against her. Slowly, she turned her head to see who it might be.

"Margaret." Even though Mary whispered, her voice sounded very loud in the dark stillness that surrounded her. "Margaret," she repeated, giving her sister's head a nudge with her shoulder.

She held her breath as she heard footsteps above her, followed by a cry of "Cast off, boys! Cast off!"

"Margaret!" Mary whispered more frantically. "Margaret." She nudged her sister who began to moan. "I think we are on a ship, Margaret. Please wake up. I cannot remain calm alone."

"A ship?" Margaret's voice was slurred.

"Are you well?"

"I cannot move my hands!" Every bit of slur was gone from Margaret's voice. She was obviously fully awake, jolted to full consciousness just as Mary had been by their shocking circumstances.

"Nor can I. We are bound and stashed in a ship. What are we to do?"

"There's not much we can do unless you can untie me, and I can untie you."

"And then what do would we do?"

"Stretch our legs," Margaret retorted. "I am most uncomfortable."

"Shhh."

Again, Mary listened to footsteps.

"We will be away from the quay soon, Sir," someone above her said.

There was a small gap above Mary, and she could just see a bit of light. Try as she might, however, she could not see more than a bit of a boot.

"When we are, I shall see to our cargo. Do you see any suspicious lights on the dock? Did anyone question your boarding?"

"No, Sir, all is quiet as it should be. No one will miss her until the sun rises."

"Good, good. I should not wish for this plan to fall apart now. Not when we have our hands on the prize." One set of footsteps departed, but Mary could still hear someone above them, shifting to and fro as if pacing a short distance and back. Something scurried across the floor near her and her sister, causing her to shudder and shift her focus from the gap overhead to her surroundings.

"Was it a rat?" Margaret whispered.

"I do not want to consider if it is or not," Mary replied. "I cannot think about that now." She was barely keeping herself from crying in fright as it was. If she were to think about some rodent running across the floor near her and possibly approaching her. She shuddered again. No, she would not think about it. She must not.

"I do not like rats," Margaret whimpered.

"No one does. Now, stop talking about rats, and do not cry. We must not cry." She could hear Margaret sniffling.

"But I am scared."

"I know," Mary moved her hands and legs so that she could pat Margaret's knee. "But we must attempt not to show it. I think these men would be happy to have us be fearful, and I do not wish to make them happy."

Margaret sniffled again. "You are right, of course, but I do not think I can be as strong as you."

"Only try."

"I will, but do not hate me if I fail."

"I could never hate you, Margaret."

"Oh, what are we going to do?"

Mary sighed and shook her head. "I do not know beyond attempting to hide our fear and not speaking of rats."

The two sisters sat silently, listening to the sounds above and around them. Despite the anxiety she felt, Mary found she could not keep her eyes from closing and her mind from drifting toward sleep. Her head hurt, and she was so tired.

"What are you doing!" Mary cried as she came entirely to her senses and tugged her feet back from the man who was pulling on them.

"I be trying to free your feet, but if you wish to remain as you are, then it is no bother to me." He folded his knife.

"Tell me why you are doing it, and I might allow you to continue."

"I ain't got to tell you nothing." The man sank back onto his heels.

"That is not what I heard your boss tell you," Margaret said before Mary could think of any reason for the man to tell her why he was attempting to free her feet.

"Is it a boss or a captain?" Margaret continued. "I am certain I do not know. We are on a ship so perhaps it must be captain. Unless, of course, he is not the captain, but he is just the man telling you what to do with the cargo. No, the cargo would be under the captain's domain, would it not?"

"Silence!" the man cried.

"I only wish to get the terminology correct," Margaret retorted.

Mary pressed her lips together. Margaret was excessively good at feigning ignorance to annoy an aggressor.

"And your boss or captain – I do not know what to call him since you will not tell me – said we were to be freed to move around our...." she paused. "I do apologize, but I am afraid I do not know what this part of a ship is called. Is it a storeroom?"

"Silence," the man growled again. "I am to free you so that you can move around this hold."

"Very well, then, you may proceed," Mary said, poking her feet toward him.

"How gracious of you," the man snarled.

"Where are we sailing to?" Margaret asked. "I have not been on a boat except to row across a pond."

"I shan't tell you no more," the man said. "I have half a mind to leave you tied up for the trouble you been."

"But then, your – captain, is it? – would not be pleased."

The man growled but said not a word.

"I truly wish you would tell me the proper word. It is most aggravating not knowing what term I should be using."

"Captain," he barked. "You may call him the captain. He be in charge of everything on this ship – including you."

"Thank you," Margaret said sweetly. "If you had just

said so to begin with, we could have avoided this whole argument. But then, you are likely not used to having ladies as cargo. At least, I should hope you are not, and I would kindly appreciate it if you would not tell me if you do have ladies as cargo on a regular basis."

"You would not like that, would you?" There was a hint of delight in the man's voice.

"Oh, 'tis not I who would not like it, although it would be most improper, especially as my sister is not married, but you would find it to be a frightfully bothersome business."

"Her husband is a parson," Mary explained as the man's brows furrowed. "My sister would feel it her duty to instruct you on your reprehensible ways."

"Oh, most certainly," Margaret cried. "Although I am not certain I can remember all the scripture as it should be read."

"And I could show you what we do with ladies who visit us," he said, leaning toward her.

"There is no need. I am certain I could tell you. Not that I will, of course."

"But can your sister?"

Mary chuckled. "I may be innocent, but I am not naive. One does not live with the admiral and remain naïve for long."

"Admiral, you say?" the man tipped his head and studied her with something that looked like respect.

"He *was* my uncle," Mary emphasized the word was. It was perhaps not a good thing for them to think she was of any sort of value besides whatever value they currently thought she was. She had no idea who these men were and for whom they sailed. "What flag are you flying?"

The man chuckled. "Not the White Ensign" was all he said before rising. "Nor the Red Ensign she normally flies."

"She is a privateer?"

"Was," he said with a laugh as he left them, locking the door behind him.

Mary stood and swung her arms back and forth while she lifted one foot and then another as if she was walking though she stood still. Then, once her arms and legs felt as if they had been loosened of the knots they had formed while she slept in such an awkward position, she moved around the small hold.

There was not much room, and what room there was was filled with crates and barrels – barrels that looked very much like the ones she had seen in Mr. Durward's warehouse. Could this be one of his boats?

She moved to look at one crate more closely. There were no markings that she recognized.

Next, she studied the lantern. The wick seemed well trimmed, and there appeared to be a good bit of oil. They should have light for some time. She tugged gently on its handle. To her relief, it was securely locked into its holder.

She widened her stance and attempted not to slide to the right as the boat rolled.

"What I would not give for a book or a bit of stitching," Margaret said.

"I do not think I could enjoy either with all this rocking," Mary said. She would do well to not become ill from the motion.

There was nothing to do besides either pace their small confines in a staggering fashion as they attempted to grow accustomed to the motion of the ship or sleep. And so, they did one for a period of time, and then endeavoured to do the other when their legs grew weary. They huddled together as comfortably as they could in a corner they created by pushing around a couple of crates. It felt secluded and gave the illusion of being safe.

Mary was not sure for how long they had slept when the sound of someone outside the locked door to their hold roused her. "Margaret," she hissed.

"What?" Margaret replied sleepily.

"We are about to have a guest."

"A guest?" Margaret's voice was panicked. "What do you think he will do with us?"

Mary pulled her self up and smoothed her skirts as much as she could. "I do not know. You did very well last time with not showing your fear, which helped me control mine. Can you do it again?" Margaret's wide, fearful eyes focused on Mary's as she nodded.

They both rose and waited for the door to open.

"Ladies."

To say that the gentleman who entered the room surprised Mary and Margaret would be too gentle a reaction. Neither lady had prepared themselves to know their captor.

"Mr. Radcliff?" Mary managed to say as Margaret clung to her arm.

"I see you remember me," Mr. Radcliff replied with a grin. "However, you may call me Captain, as this is my boat."

"Your boat?" Mary repeated.

"Yes, my boat, though we have been separated these three years." He pulled over a crate and tipped it on its side. "Please be seated."

Mary was grateful for the makeshift bench for her legs had gone wobbly at his entrance.

"It will be good to see her home again instead of in English hands."

"You are not British?"

He cursed in French. "I am only British to win back my lady." He patted the side of the hull. "It was good of Durward to give her to me." He chuckled. "His partners will not be pleased I suppose, but then they are already not pleased with him." He turned and leaned against the wall. "It seems privateering comes easily as stealing is second nature to him."

"I cannot believe that!" Margaret cried.

Again, Radcliff laughed. "He is very good at concealing it. However, he has been skimming money from his partners for some time, and they are just now finding out about it. He will not like how that turns out, but then, he has greater things to worry about than that." He shifted from leaning on one foot to the other. "He was arrested earlier today for pinching a piece of jewelry from Lady St. James. I understand she insulted him once, and he wished to take his revenge. He'll likely hang. It is why I had to reclaim my lady before we had planned. I could not count on the assistance of a dead man."

Mary clutched her throat. It could not be true. She must consider who was telling her these things. Mr. Radcliff had had her and her sister kidnapped. He was not to be trusted. Mr. Durward was. She repeated this to herself.

"Why are we travelling with you?" Margaret asked.

"Frenchmen – at least, the ones I know and work with – adore British ladies, but if they do not want you, I am certain your brother or husband would pay handsomely to have your returned." He grimaced. "I had hoped that Durward would be the one paying the ransom – I saw how sweet he was on you, Miss Crawford, but then he got caught. So, I do hope for your sakes there are those who would wish to see you returned."

"We are going to France?" Mary managed to ask.

Radcliff nodded.

"Mr. Durward is in prison?" Margaret asked.

Again, Radcliff nodded. "It's here in the paper." He pulled an article from his pocket. "I apologize, but I spilled wine on the bottom half that tells of where he is being held."

Mary scanned the news account about Lady St. James reporting a theft and then the few snatches of what she could read beyond that mentioned something about Mr. Durward having the brooch. It could not be true. It could not be. And yet, here it was in black and white.

Radcliff took the paper from her lap. "I will have some blankets and such sent to you along with some food. I apologize that the accommodations cannot be more to your normal standard, but I cannot risk losing such valuable cargo. My friends would be very upset if I were to lose you. You understand, of course."

He did not wait to allow them to reply but left quickly, locking the door behind him.

Chapter 13

"What are you doing standing on the street?" Gabe inquired of his mother when he finally reached his home later that evening well after the sun had disappeared behind the horizon. "You will catch a chill." She was not accustomed to the weather in England yet. She was always cold and yet, here she was standing in front of his house with little more than a shawl to keep her warm.

"You did not come home for dinner," she scolded as he wrapped his greatcoat around her and ushered her back toward the house.

"I was busy." He had been riding up and down streets for hours in an attempt to find any sign of Mary.

"Mr. Bertram is here."

"And he allowed you to stand out here?"

"He does not know I was outside. Do not blame him for my need to see if you were returning home or not. A mother worries when her son does not come home when he is expected."

"I apologize, Mama. I should have come home for dinner and then returned to my business."

"Of chasing after nothing?"

He had seen that look from her many times when she was not pleased with him.

"I was not chasing after nothing."

"You are if you have no direction in which to look."

"And how was I supposed to find the direction in which to look?" He followed her down the corridor to the sitting room.

"Mr. Crawford is also here," she said over her shoulder.

"Does he have any news?"

"No, but Mr. Newman does."

Gabe stopped mid-stride. Mr. Newman was at his house? They had not asked for the books to be returned until tomorrow. Surely, there was no way they had sent someone to claim them early or worse — to present him with their accusations.

His mother poked her head out of the sitting room door. "Are you coming?"

He hurried to her. As it happened, it was not just Mr. Crawford, Tom, and Mr. Newman who were in his sitting room with his mother. There were also three others — Mr. Terrell, Mr. Waller, and Mr. Fitzroy, all of whom were amongst his partners. No wonder his mother was particularly anxious to have him home.

"How may I be of service?" he said, taking a seat near

the fire as his mother was motioning him to do. To be honest, the heat was not unwelcome. He had grown somewhat chilled while riding.

"Did you find anything?" Henry asked.

Gabe shook his head and took the glass of rum his mother offered him. Out of the corner of his eye, he could see that Tom was attempting not to grin at the coddling Gabe was receiving. A quick look around the group let him know that it was not just Tom who was finding it amusing. He sighed, resigning himself to the embarrassment. There was no way he was going to tell his mother not to care for him. His mother was one of the more demonstrative and outspoken sorts of ladies, and if he tried to protest her care, she would counter his protests and the embarrassment would be multiplied.

"I am sorry I cannot be the bearer of better news," he said to Henry. "How is Dr. Grant?"

"He is resting as well as can be expected."

"It was not an apoplexy, then?"

Henry shook his head. "No. Although the physician has given him some tinctures as well as some strict instructions for rest."

"But he will rest better if we find his wife."

Henry nodded his agreement to Gabe's statement.

"And how might I be of service to the rest of you gentlemen? I have the accounts if that is what you wish to collect. I am not in a state to be of any good at finding an error tonight, so if you take them now, it will save you a trip tomorrow."

Mr. Newman drew his head back as his brow furrowed. "I do not have the pleasure of understanding your meaning."

"Mr. Radcliff gave me a message that you would send someone to collect the ledgers in the morning. It was at the same time when he collected my key from me and sent me packing."

"Sent you packing?" Mr. Terrell cried.

Gabe swallowed the last of his rum and shrugged off the blanket his mother had placed on his knees. "I am to remain at home until you have decided what to do with me and the error I have discovered."

"Who decided that?" Mr. Fitzroy asked.

"Mr. Radcliff said it was a group decision." A sense of dread was beginning to settle into Gabe's stomach. "Was that not true?"

"It is the first I have heard of it," said Mr. Waller.

"But it does explain why I heard you had left the warehouse looking offended," added Mr. Newman. "And it might explain what I am about to tell you as well." The man shifted and looked uneasily at his companions.

Apparently, whatever Mr. Newman had to say was going to take some restraint to receive with any amount of equanimity in front of his mother.

"We had a report that a ship of yours has been," he shrugged, "moved."

"Moved? From one place to another at the quay?"

Mr. Waller shook his head. "From one port to another is the apparent plan."

"One of my ships has been stolen?" Gabe shot from his seat to pace the room.

Mr. Newman nodded. "The *Edie*. I was given the report half an hour ago."

The *Edie*, a fast and maneuverable brig which had done well for him both in prize expeditions and when delivering goods, had been Gabe's first prize – his first token of success in his new life of independence from the company.

"You heard a half hour ago?" His supper was destined to be ignored tonight, for he was convinced that it was possible to catch his ship. Moving quickly down the crowded Thames in a ship the size of the *Edie* was not possible, even at night. He had no idea what he would do once he caught her, but that did not matter. She had been stolen, and, consequently, her recovery had to be attempted.

Therefore, thirty minutes later, he had sent a message to round up a crew of six sturdy rowers who were not afraid of a skirmish, kissed his mother good-bye, and was at the dock, climbing into a rowboat with a crew of half-sober, armed men to help him navigate through the thick traffic on the river in pursuit of his boat.

As he was settling into his seat, Mr. Waller climbed in beside him.

"Keeping an eye on me for the others?" Gabe asked.

Waller shook his head. "I'm joining you of my own accord. I've been on plenty of captures, and nearly had the running of my own vessel until I learned of your partnership and saw a way to earn my keep without risking my own life and limb to do so."

Gabe lifted a brow in question.

Waller shrugged. "I wish to marry."

Gabe understood that motive for leaving adventure behind for something more sedate. However, at present part of his livelihood, which would allow him to marry, was sailing down the Thames, and the lady to whom he wished to be wed was missing somewhere in London.

"Do you have a lady in mind for the position of Mrs. Waller?" Gabe asked as he, Waller, and the rowers began to move the boat away from its mooring.

"I do. A pretty thing she is too, and she'll be mine as soon as I can set myself up well enough to please her father."

The oars sliced through the water as some of the men sang to keep the rhythm steady.

"This will be a dangerous adventure," Gabe cautioned Waller.

"I know, Durward. I have heard that you are not one to be crossed, and since I am experienced, I figured my assistance might prove beneficial." He grinned at Gabe. "And I cannot deny that I want to see if the stories I have heard of you are correct."

"Stories?" Gabe feigned ignorance. He had a good idea what sorts of stories Waller had likely been told.

"I heard you've taken on a fellow or two who have tried to take advantage of you, and there are many around the docks who respect you as only they will for a man they know will do exactly as he says he will." He chuckled. "I understand those men who attempted to play you false are no longer in England proper."

"You heard well," Gabe replied.

"That is why the others are so anxious about the books," he said.

"What do you mean?"

"Not one of them thinks you would pilfer money, and they are each hoping it does not appear to be them who is at fault."

"Then they are not going to accuse me of taking the missing funds?"

Waller shook his head. "There might be one or two who have not heeded the others, but the majority of us are not looking at you as the source of the trouble. And now with this taking place tonight, I think we will have our man."

"Radcliff," Gabe growled the name.

Waller nodded. "Dreadfully annoying fellow."

"No truer words have been spoken."

The men fell back into silence for a time as they concentrated on taking strong strokes, urging their boat to cut through the water as fast as possible.

"I'll board first," Gabe said as they approached the *Edie*. He made certain his gun was loaded, and his knife was within reach. Then he began scaling the vessel as quietly as he could.

Waller and the others were to follow.

"I'd not go any further."

Gabe, who had just gotten to his feet after boarding the ship, spun about to see Radcliff aiming a gun at him.

"You thought you could take her from me again?" Radcliff sneered. "I say," he took a step closer to Gabe as a few crew members formed a circle about him. "I thought you might attempt it, so I prepared." He stepped to the side and, making a sweeping motion with his pistol, directed Gabe's attention to the door to the lower deck where Mary and Margaret were being held with knives to their throats. "You can have one lady," he said, "but not all three."

Gabe's heart dropped to his boots, and he rushed toward Radcliff. However, three crewmen stopped him.

"With which one will you leave?" Radcliff was close enough for Gabe to smell the rum on the man's breath. "Mrs. Grant, Miss Crawford, or your beloved ship?"

Gabe struggled against the men holding him, and one gave way, causing Radcliff to scamper backward, spewing a litany of French curses as he did. If only Gabe could lose the other two, he was confident he could take Radcliff. The man was small and apparently not as brave as he acted.

"I am not leaving." Gabe walked forward, slowly, straining against the two men who attempted to keep him back. "You may keep both me and my ship. The ladies will be leaving."

"No!" Mary cried.

"Let me talk to her." Gabe stopped straining against his captors as he waited for Radcliff to reply. "Just to say my farewell," he added. He needed to be able to send her home to safety. Nothing else mattered to him at that moment other than seeing her safe.

Radcliff smiled. "You know you'll not reach France alive."

"Or you won't," Gabe replied.

"One of you against my crew of many?" Radcliff scoffed.

Apparently, Waller had yet to be noticed, or the man had not boarded behind him. Of course, even with Waller and his rowers, they would be outnumbered two to one.

"Do you ladies know how to row?" Radcliff laughed at the thought. "I think my offer stands as stated since I do not intend to allow you to live anyway." He shrugged. "In fact, when you are dead, who's to say I must let either of them go?"

"You do not need them. I have money. I can get you what you want."

"I already have what I want," Radcliff replied.

"It will not go well for you, if you are caught," Gabe said as calmly as he could. "Murderers are not dealt with gently."

"You are not in a position to bargain with me," Radcliff shouted. "You think you are in control of all things. You and your money!"

Gabe's brows furrowed. Whatever was he talking about?

"Safety! Insurance!" Radcliff shook his head and approached Gabe again. "I could have taken more than this one boat back to France if you had not been so determined to have a larger crew on board the next venture."

Ah! The angry little Frenchman was beginning to make sense.

"You were the only one to hold out. You, who had stolen my boat." Radcliff shook his head and laughed menacingly. "Take the ladies below!" he barked. "Unless they would like to witness Mr. Durward's demise."

"No!" Mary cried again.

"Please, let me talk to her," Gabe begged, wanting desperately to tell her he loved her one time before it was too late. He did not plan on dying easily, but he also knew his survival was not guaranteed.

"Take her below!" Radcliff yelled.

Gabe attempted to shake his captors from him, but to

no avail, as Mary and Margaret were taken below once again.

"You may leave him to me now," he said to his men as the door to the lower deck closed with a heavy thud, and he drew back the hammer on his pistol.

Chapter 14

"I will not go back in there!" Mary rooted her feet to the deck and folded her arms.

"You'll go where I say." The man holding her upper arm placed the tip of his knife under her chin. "Or you'll die."

"We can't kill them unless Radcliff says." The other man dragged Margaret over near Mary, so he could give his companion a shove. "She's but a slip of a thing. Just move her and be done."

The tip of Mary's captor's knife pressed more firmly into the underside of her chin. "You be lucky I can't do as I wish," he snarled. Then, putting his knife away, he pushed her into the hold.

Mary stumbled and fell just as she heard a shot ring out overhead.

"No!" she wailed, scrambling to her feet. He couldn't be dead. Mr. Durward could not be dead!

She banged at the door. She shouted at the ceiling. She fell against the door, breathing heavily, and attempting not to succumb to the great sobs that she could feel fighting to be given freedom.

"You are bleeding." Margaret pressed her handkerchief to Mary's chin. "Come. Sit with me."

Mary allowed herself to be moved from the door. "What will I do without him?" she whispered as she pulled Margaret's handkerchief from her chin and looked at the small crimson stain on it before returning it to her chin.

"You were set against him just moments ago."

Mary leaned heavily into her sister's side when Margaret wrapped an arm around her shoulders.

"He is not in prison," Mary answered. Moments ago, before those two men had come to haul her and Margaret to the deck above, she had thought Mr. Durward was in prison. Now, he was dead. Lying on the deck above them. Dead. None of what had troubled her before mattered. Not the tales about his thefts. Not his exotic mistress. Nothing. He was dead, and he would never be hers. And the pain of that was far more overwhelming than the pain she had felt when considering him untrustworthy.

"I believe I told you not to believe that," Margaret said softly. "You were looking for reasons to doubt him."

Her mind had told her that Mr. Radcliff had fabricated at least part of his story. That was what had made the pain bearable before – there was still hope that she was wrong and Mr. Durward was a worthy suitor to whom she could trust her heart. Now, she knew that worthy or not, he had claimed her heart. There was no way she was going to be parted from him in any fashion that would not result in the greatest sorrow. Mary took a shuddering breath as tears finally slid down her cheeks.

"You were fearful of being hurt. That is not unnatural." Margaret's voice was soft and soothing.

"What does it matter now?" Mary managed to rasp out between sobs. How could her sister be so calm at a moment like this? Up until now, her sister had been anxious at every sound.

"Are you listening?"

Mary nodded. Perhaps it was just that her sister knew how best to comfort her and had pushed her fears aside to do so. It would be very like Margaret to do that.

"I do not think you are."

Mary looked at the handkerchief she held. The bleeding from the cut on her chin seemed to have stopped, so she used it to dry her cheeks. "Then say what you said again, but I am certain I heard it all."

"No, I do not mean are you listening to me. Can you not hear the shouting above us?"

Mary shook her head. There was no shouting. Was there? Her eyes grew wide as the noise of a scuffle and shouts were heard above her.

"Have faith," Margaret whispered. "We must have faith that just as what Mr. Radcliff claimed about Mr. Durward being in prison was untrue, what we heard above us was not what we think we heard."

"You think he is alive?"

Margaret shrugged, and tears glistened in her eyes. "I do not know, but perhaps he is?"

That would have to be enough. Mary would have to cling to the hope that Mr. Durward might be alive. She dried her eyes and nose and rose. If there was a chance that someone might still hear her, she was not going to wait quietly.

"We are in the hold!" she shouted to the crack in the ceiling before turning to pound on the door again.

As she walked between the door and that hole through which she could see just a few stars to repeat her actions, the door opened. Expectantly, Mary spun towards it only to be disappointed to find it was not Mr. Durward. It was the same fellow who had cut the ropes off them earlier.

"Quickly," he said with a nervous look over his shoulder. "Come." He waved them toward himself.

"Why?" Margaret asked. "Where are you taking us?"

"I am setting you free," he replied with a more frantic wave for them to come with him. "There weren't supposed to be no killing."

Mary gasped. He was dead. She knew it!

"Just kidnapping?" Margaret asked in a sardonic tone.

"I be helping you. Shut up." He stalked out of the room. "Stay in there if you wish. Ain't none of my problem now.

Thought you might want to leave with that fellow." He waved his hand at the deck overhead.

"He's alive?" Mary ran out of the room and grabbed their rescuer by his arm. "Mr. Durward is alive?"

"Might be. Last I saw, he was bleeding less than the captain." He covered one of Mary's hand with one of his. "You will tell them that I helped you?"

"Who?"

"That man and the others what came for you."

"Of course. I will tell the truth."

"'Twasn't me that snatched you neither. I just cut your ropes and opened the door for you. Was them other two with the knives what knocked you on the head and stashed you in there." He jutted his chin toward the hold.

"But you stole his ship," Margaret said.

"I ain't took nothing. I was hired to help sail her. That is all."

"You knew it was stolen," Margaret insisted.

The man scowled. "I could lock ye up again."

"Stealing is wrong. So is locking people up."

"Shut up," the man spat at her. "Be careful exiting at the top of the ladder. They be a few still scrapping." And with that, he left them and ducked into some room down the hall.

Mary poked her head out of the door to the main deck first. There were still a few men fighting. She looked one direction and then the other. She could not see Mr. Durward anywhere. Quietly, she stepped out, still uncertain of which way she should go. Mr. Durward had been standing in front of her and to the left. Therefore, his boat must be there.

Mary grasped Margaret's hand, and together they hurried in the direction where Mary thought they might find Mr. Durward's boat.

As they approached the stern of the ship, Mary covered her mouth to keep from crying out. In front of them, Mr. Durward lay on the deck, sprawled in a most lifeless position. Dropping her sister's hand, she ran to him and fell to her knees beside him.

He opened his eyes and smiled at her before they fluttered shut again.

"So very touching."

Mary froze at the sound of Radcliff's voice. Slowly, she turned to look at him. He was leaning heavily on some piece of the boat which Mary could not identify. His jacket and breeches were stained with blood, and his face was ashen.

Mr. Durward's hand grasped hers, causing her attention to be drawn back to him.

"My gun," he whispered. "Where is it?"

Mary looked around.

"What? Are you going to ignore me?" Radcliff shouted.

"Beside your left hand," Mary answered Mr. Durward while attempting to ignore Mr. Radcliff.

"Fall on my chest and do not move until I say."

"Why?"

"Just trust me." He drew a breath with effort. "And tell your sister to come toward my head."

Mary looked at Margaret and motioned for her to move forward a bit. "Stay by his head."

"I will not be ignored!" Radcliff yelled.

Mary heard the unmistakable sound of a sword being unsheathed.

"Fall on me."

Mary threw herself on top of Mr. Durward and lay there, holding her breath with her eyes closed, startling only slightly as the sound of a gun being fired rattled her brain.

Then, something heavy fell on her, and Mr. Durward cursed.

"May I move?" Margaret asked.

"Get him off of her!" Mr. Durward said.

Him? Mary glanced over her shoulder to see that Mr. Radcliff was the heavy object which had fallen on her.

"Remove his sword from my leg." The words were said with effort.

As soon as Mary was freed from the weight of Mr. Radcliff, she did as instructed and removed the sword from where it pinned Mr. Durward's breeches to the deck. A red splotch spread across the area.

Mr. Durward grasped her hand. "You are safe now."

She nodded as tears filled her eyes.

He smiled once more before his eyes fluttered closed and did not reopen. Mary fell on his chest once more. Her tears soaking his jacket as she listened for a heartbeat. It was there, but it was not strong.

"Please," she pleaded. "Do not die."

"Miss."

"Crawford," Margaret said. "And I am Mrs. Grant, her sister."

"Mr. Waller, one of Mr. Durward's partners," Mary heard whoever it was that had joined them say.

"It will take some time to get this ship back to the quay. If you are not afraid to do so, you can return to the shore in the rowboat with Mr. Durward. It is a faster way to travel."

"Miss Crawford?" Mr. Waller crouched near her. "Does he live?"

Mary nodded.

"Will you travel with him?"

Again, Mary nodded.

"Then allow us to prepare him for the journey."

Mary slowly rose from where she was but did not move far from Mr. Durward as several men tied bandages around his wounds and prepared ropes to lower him down to the boat below.

"You will need to wait until we have secured him in the boat," Mr. Waller said.

"Of course." She watched as men climbed over the rails and down the ladder to the rowboat. It appeared as if there was not one of them who was not wearing some sort of injury. Even Mr. Waller, who stood with her, had blood on his sleeve and a bruised eye and lip.

"His mother will be happy to have him returned," Mr. Waller said conversationally.

Mary smiled politely. She knew he was only trying to distract her from what was happening.

"You should have seen her earlier," he continued. "We were at Durward's home to tell him about the missing ship, and she was up and out of the door more than once to see if he was home yet." He leaned toward her a bit. "He was out looking for you."

"He was?"

Mr. Waller nodded. "And when he finally arrived, his mother sat about tucking him into a chair near the fire. I admit I found it humorous to see Durward being so cosseted. And by such a little lady at that!"

Mary could not help but smile at the image. She would very much like to see Mr. Durward being cared for in such a fashion.

"Have you met his mother?"

Mary shook her head. "Not yet."

"You will like her. She is quite the lady!" He motioned toward the rail. "It is time."

Margaret climbed over first, though it took some encouragement from Mary to do so. Then, it was Mary's turn.

As she looked down at the black water, she knew precisely why Margaret had been so hesitant. It was a long way down to that rowboat, and neither ship nor rowboat wished to remain standing still. Yet, as she saw Mr. Durward, swaddled in a blanket laying there below her, she knew she could push those fears of falling aside and make the descent. She stepped to the rail, attempted to climb over as gracefully as she could, and began to climb down. But then, remembering something, she returned to the top of the ladder.

"Mr. Waller," she called.

"Yes," he said, coming to where she was at the rail.

"There is a man below deck who helped us. He was the one assigned to cut our ropes and then when things were going poorly up here, he came down and opened the door, so we could go free. I told him I would tell you what he had done." She shrugged. "In case, it will help his cause."

"Do you know his name?"

Mary shook her head. "I am afraid I do not. However, if you begin speaking about my sister, he'll likely be the first to curse."

Mr. Waller chuckled. "Thank you, Miss Crawford, and I applaud you. Not many would delay their departure to help someone who had been part of their need for rescue. I will make a note of your report and make certain all the necessary officials know about it."

Mary thanked him and once again pushed her fear of

falling into the cold dark water below out of her mind as she climbed down to the safety of the boat below her and to the man who held her heart and whose heart, she hoped, still beat within his chest.

Chapter 15

The smell of the river was the first thing that penetrated Gabe's senses, causing him to stir. He groaned as he tried to move. Why did his body hurt as it did? And what was pressing on his chest? He attempted to open his eyes, but all that moved were his eyebrows.

"Shhh. Rest quietly."

The heaviness on his chest lifted, but instead of feeling relieved, he missed the warm, protection of whatever it was. Or whoever it was, he adjusted as a hand cupped his cheek.

"We will be to the dock soon."

He attempted to open his eyes again, but they still would not allow him to look at the lovely lady who was now stroking his forehead.

"Rest," Mary cooed.

A drop of something wet splashed on his cheek and was quickly brushed away. Sniffling. She was crying. He forced his eyes to open enough so that he could see her through his lashes. If he could get his arms out from under these blankets, he could touch her, and she would know she had nothing to fear. But he could not do more than lift his hand and place it on his stomach under the blankets.

Thankfully, she must have either felt or seen him move, for she covered his hand with hers. How he loved the feeling of her being so near, of her administering caresses and whispers, and of her grasping his hand. It was as if she belonged to him. In his heart she did, but he had yet to persuade her into accepting him.

"Rest," she cooed to him once again.

"My mother," he whispered but found he had little strength to continue. He wanted to explain to her what she had seen the other day.

"She will be happy to see you," Mary replied, "but please rest. We can speak when you are safe."

The heaviness on his chest returned, and he could faintly smell her. Her hand still held his while her ear lay over his heart. He breathed in as deeply as he could and allowed his tired mind and body to sleep. He was unaware of anything but the wonderful dream of Mary resting on his chest until the warm protection of her presence abandoned him, and the blanket on which he lay began to be lifted.

He groaned as he was jostled by the moving from boat to shore.

"Be careful with him."

His lips curled upward. She was still seeing to his care.

"It seems we have a welcoming party waiting for us," said one of the men standing near Gabe's head.

Gabe opened his eyes, hoping to catch a glimpse of whoever it was that was here to greet him. But it was useless. All he could see were the edges of the blanket and the men carrying him. None of them looked to be in perfect condition. There were bruised faces and bloodied clothing.

And then there was her face. She was following at his feet. Her face also had blood on it, but he supposed it was not hers, but his, that stained her and made her more beautiful to him, for it spoke of her care. He smiled when she saw that he was awake, and his heart beat a little stronger when she returned the smile. He could stay on shore and far from the interest of the city if he could see her smile at him always. There was nothing, absolutely nothing, that he desired more than her.

"My son!"

Of course, it was his mother who was at the dock in the middle of the night, waiting for him to return. That woman was determined to catch her death of cold at his expense. If he had the strength, he would scold her, but as he did not, he would simply wait to be accosted by her reprimands for how he must look.

"There is a cart just next to the warehouse."

Mr. Newman was here with his mother?

"We can use one of my horses to pull it."

Tom was here as well?

"Mary! Margaret!"

It seemed the whole party from his sitting room earlier tonight was here.

"Go to him," Gabe said as he saw Mary smile at her brother but not leave her place at his feet.

She shook her head until he frowned. Then, she did as he said. He could well imagine the happy relief that Mr. Crawford must be feeling.

"Are you injured?" Gabe heard Henry ask his sister.

"It is only a small cut."

She was injured? He jerked his head around to try to see her. It was a foolish, painful action, but he needed to know how and where she had been injured.

"This is mostly from Mr. Durward. My scratch is nothing."

"It is not a scratch," he heard Margaret correct Mary.

"Then what is it?" Henry demanded.

"The work of a knife is what it is!" Margaret cried.

"It is tiny," Mary protested.

"Where?" Gabe asked one of the men at his head.

"Where what?"

"Her injury?"

The man chuckled. "Whoever he is is examining her chin." He pointed to a place on his own face, just behind his jawbone. "I had not noticed it, so I am certain it is small just as she said."

They walked on for a few steps before the man added.

"It's likely the scoundrel who gave her that cut has either breathed his last or will at the end of a rope."

Gabe nodded. They understood each other. No matter how insignificant an injury a lady received, men such as they would wish to see it redressed.

"Oh, my son!"

They must be close to the warehouse, for his mother was now at his side, squeezing in between the gentlemen who carried him.

"What have you done to yourself?" She shook her head and clucked her tongue, despite the tears that spilled down her face.

"I will be well, Mama," he assured her.

"How can you say that? You are being carried by six men. You are not well."

"He will be," Tom pulled Gabe's mom away. "They need to load him into the cart. It is time we leave so that we can prepare for his arrival at home."

"Can I not ride in the cart?" she asked.

"No," Tom replied. "You will want his bed ready, and those men will need to ride somewhere as we will need them to carry him into the house since I do not think either you or I will be able to do it."

"But he is my boy."

Gabe rolled his eyes as the men carrying him chuckled.

"We have all had mothers at one point or another," one of the men assured him. "And then when we think we are rid of them, we get a wife to take up where our mothers left off." A laugh rippled through the group.

With any luck, Gabe would have both a mother and a wife to torture him with their care. "Miss Crawford," he said as the last man was climbing in next to him.

"I am here."

Those were perhaps the most precious words he had ever heard.

"I will call on you tomorrow. Henry knows where you live." Her eyes glistened, but she smiled. Then, she stepped back, and the cart began its bumpy journey.

"It was his mother," he heard her say to someone — most likely her sister. He sighed in relief. He would rest much more easily knowing that she knew the truth.

~*~*~

"Before my mother returns," Gabe said to Tom later, after Gabe had been cleaned up, the surgeon had done his work, and Gabe had been fed some broth, "would you bring me that ring I showed you?"

Tom smiled. "You are not waiting until you are healed."

Gabe shook his head. "I came very close to dying tonight – not that you are to tell my mother that."

Tom laughed.

"One does not wait to do anything after he has barely escaped the cold clutches of death," Gabe continued. "And I do believe Miss Crawford might actually be willing to accept me even in my broken condition."

There was a knock at the door before his mother entered.

"You should be sleeping." She crossed to the room to sit on the foot of his bed. "So many bandages." She shook her head. "And for a boat."

"Not just a boat," Gabe answered. "It was at first, but then when I saw Miss Crawford and her sister being held with knives to their throats, I no longer cared one wit about that boat. What is a man's livelihood if it comes at the expense of his heart?"

His mother smiled. "She is very pretty."

"Did you speak to her?"

His mother shook her head. "She was busy with her brother, and I had you." She sighed. "I suppose I shall not have you much longer."

"I am not planning to die."

"No, but you will marry."

"And you will still be my mother. I am not sending you away."

"Ah, but I shall have to mind my place."

Gabe chuckled. "I do not think it possible," he teased. "You will like her, Mama, and she will like you."

His mother looked down at the bed and played with the blanket. "I hope you are correct."

"She is coming to call tomorrow."

His mother fiddled some more with the blanket and did not raise her eyes.

"When was the last time I lied to you?"

That startled his mother enough for her to look at him.

"I cannot remember when it was," she answered.

"And I am not lying to you now. I am certain Miss Crawford will like you."

"You make it very hard for one not to like you," Tom added, earning a smile from Gabe's mom. "I hear the young lady sustained an injury while on board that ship."

Gabe closed his eyes and shook his head. He did not know if he was grateful or perturbed with Tom for stirring his mother's curiosity.

"How did that happen?" she asked.

"I do not know. I only know that she has a small cut on her chin from a knife," Gabe replied. "We will have to ask her tomorrow."

"I should like to know the story," his mother replied.

"All stories will have to wait until tomorrow," Gabe said, "for I will need a night of rest before I am ready to share any of what I remember of tonight with anyone."

"Well," said Tom rising, "I will get that item you requested and leave it with your man, and then, I shall go home for a good rest so that I am prepared to hear all the shocking details on the morrow."

He paused for a moment next to Gabe's bed and looked down at him. "I am very happy that I will have the opportunity to hear the details from your lips and not another's."

Gabe nodded his understanding. He was equally as happy to be alive to share the details.

"I will leave you when you are sleeping." His mother ran a hand up and down the lower portion of the leg that was near her.

He had known she would be reluctant to leave him. He could not blame her. Truth be told, he was happy to have her stay and give him some comfort. "Pull that chair up here and hold my hand."

She scooted to do as he asked, settling into the chair and smiling happily as she took his hand.

He squeezed that comforting hand. "I will tell you this much about tonight because I think it will help you feel more at ease about Miss Crawford." He sighed. "As far as I can tell, Miss Crawford travelled from my ship to the dock with her head resting on my chest to listen to my heart."

His mother gasped softly and brushed at the tears that gathered on her lower lashes. She lifted his hand and kissed it. "You have found a very good lady."

He nodded. He had. Miss Crawford was the perfect lady for him.

His mother settled back into the chair and rested her head against the wing of the back as she held his hand. "She will care for you very well," she whispered. "This is very good."

In that moment, Gabe realized that his mother's anxiety in meeting Miss Crawford was not just because she feared that Miss Crawford would not like her or that she would not like Miss Crawford. It was as it always was with his mother. She was concerned that he was well. Gabe squeezed her hand and closed his eyes, hoping to dream of that very good lady of whom his mother already most heartily approved.

Chapter 16

"And that is when I saw Miss Crawford and Mrs. Grant were on board the ship." Gabe paused in his tale, to take a sip of tea.

Mary's heart raced even now, remembering that moment. She could still feel the cool edge of the knife against her neck and smell the foul odor of the man holding her. She was sure he had not seen a speck of soap in several weeks. But it was not the rank filthiness of the man nor the threat of harm which had caused her to feel as if she would faint dead away.

She drew a breath and quietly sighed as she shared a smile with Mr. Durward. He was alive, and though he appeared somewhat battered and bruised, he looked as if he was doing well for someone who had come so close to death's door. She pressed her lips together and glanced down at her cup of tea. She had no desire to cry in a room filled with so many people.

"Were you not frightened?" Gabe's mother directed her question to Mary and Margaret.

"Terrified," Margaret answered, "and not just for ourselves. Your son offered his life in exchange for ours!"

Mary watched horror battle with pride in the lady's eyes.

"I could do no less."

His mother sighed and nodded as if she knew it was true. A small smile tipped her lips, and she seemed content with the answer. It was amazing to Mary to witness a relationship such as Gabe had with his mother. It was so foreign to her. If Mary had not already come to know that she could trust Mr. Durward, she would have been thoroughly won over by watching him here today with his mother. They seemed to understand and respect each other, and even when there were small disagreements – over things such as if Gabe had enough blankets – they did not dissolve into fits of pique or harsh words. One or the other would simply choose to defer to the other.

"And then we were hauled below – and none too gently, mind you," Margaret continued. "And that is when Mary received that gash on her chin."

"It is not a gash!" Mary cried.

Mrs. Durward opened her mouth as if she wished to say something and then thinking better of it closed it again.

Gabe chuckled. "I think you should show your wound to us so that we may judge if it is you or your sister who is correct."

"It did not even require a stitch," Mary protested. "It can barely be claimed as an injury."

"Had it not come at the end of some fiendish man's knife, I might allow that to be true," Margaret said.

Mary sighed.

"I know I'd like to see it," Gabe said.

Embarrassment painted Mary's cheeks as she tipped her head back to expose the underside of her chin to the group. "He only pierced the skin. It is no bigger than a prick."

"It is very red," Mrs. Durward said. "It might require a poultice to keep it from getting infected. Infection needs only a tiny opening to set about its dangerous work, you know."

"It does look a little angry," Gabe agreed with a smile for Mary when she returned her head to its proper position.

"It is sore," Mary admitted sheepishly.

Mrs. Durward, who was sitting on Mary's right while Gabe was on Mary's left, placed a hand on Mary's arm. "You will put something on it when you return home, will you not?"

Mary nodded. "Margaret will see that I do."

"She is a good sister to you," Mrs. Durward added.

Mary could not help how fond she was growing of Mrs. Durward. The lady was a small bundle of energy, fueled, it seemed, by motherly care for everyone she met. She had insisted on Mary and Margaret sitting nearest the hearth. Tom appeared to be much like a second son to the lady, and she had inquired after Mr. Waller's comfort several times as well as Henry's, although Mr. Waller looked as if he needed care a lot more than Henry did.

"How did you escape Mr. Radcliff's gun?" Mary asked Gabe.

"Waller."

"The other men and I had crept aboard the ship while Durward had Radcliff and his men's attention." Mr. Waller sighed. "Had my aim been better, the battle would have been over much sooner than it was. I missed my mark but a few inches." He pointed to his chest and then moved his finger to his left shoulder as he spoke indicating both where he had aimed and where he actually hit.

"I am thankful for the shot no matter where it hit Radcliff," Gabe said plainly.

"It was fortunate your shot was better than mine," Waller replied.

Gabe nodded. "I am not saying your incentive for accuracy was not great, Waller, but I think mine was far greater." He took Mary's hand, causing her to blush and dip her head.

"I would not disagree with such a claim," Waller said.

Tom stood. "I should likely contrive some reason to persuade you all to leave the room and allow Gabe and Miss Crawford some privacy, but I have not been able to come up with one. Therefore, I suggest we all take our leave and perhaps enjoy another cup of tea in the morning room."

Mary thought her cheeks were about to burst into

flames from discomposure while her heart would leap from her chest in delight.

"We could play cards," Mrs. Durward suggested. Then with what Mary imagined was a motherly pat of reassurance on Mary's arm, the lady rose and led the group from the room.

"That was not done with any great amount of grace, but it was effective," Gabe said as Tom closed the door to the sitting room. "And I suppose it will make it more obvious and humiliating if you refuse me."

Mary shook her head. "I will not refuse."

Gabe chuckled. "You have not heard my offer. I might be asking you to be my scullery maid," he teased.

"Would you visit me in the kitchen every day?" Mary asked playfully.

"I would likely spend my entire day in the kitchen if you were there," he replied.

"Then, I would still not refuse. However, your cook would probably send me packing within a fortnight, if she allowed me to stay that long." She lifted the hand that held hers and kissed it.

"You would scrub dishes in my kitchen if I asked you to do so?" His voice had turned soft and quiet.

"You offered your life and your ship to save my life and that of my sister, I would do anything you asked me to do." Tears filled her eyes. How easily they sprang up now that she had found a reason to no longer guard her heart so fiercely.

"So it would be out of duty – some sort of repayment?" His left brow arched but his lips curled into a smile as if he knew what her answer would be.

"No." She said only that one word and returned his smile. If he was going to lead her down some merry path, she was not going to deny either him or herself the pleasure.

"Then what would it be?" He shifted in his chair so that he was closer to her. "Blasted injuries," he grumbled. "I would rather be much closer to you than I am."

Mary released his hand and, rising, pushed her chair closer to his.

"I did not even ask, and yet, you have done what I wish," he teased while reaching forward to see if he could touch her cheek.

Mary pressed herself close to the arm of the chair. Still, it was not quite enough to allow him to touch her without straining.

He tipped his head and looked at her.

"What are you thinking?" she asked cautiously.

"It is most improper, but I was thinking that my lap is not broken. My stitches are in my arm and the lower portion of my leg. The rest of me is battered and sore, but you would do me no harm if you were to join me in my chair."

"I fear if we are discovered, there will be a price to pay," Mary teased.

"Are you afraid to pay it?"

Mary shook her head and moved to perch gently on his lap. It was most improper and yet pleasantly so. She attempted to relax and snuggle into his embrace when he wrapped his unbandaged arm around her and pulled her close.

"Now, why do you not tell me why you would do whatever it is that I ask of you?"

Her cheeks flushed at his deeper tone of voice. An innocent she might be, but naïve, she was not. She hoped that her own voice would not carry too much of her desire for him when she spoke. However, she was not able to hide it all, and as she spoke, he wrapped his arm around her more tightly.

"I know that you would never allow me to take on water – I believe that is how you said it."

He chuckled. "It is."

"I have nothing to fear from you, Mr. Durward."

"You are sitting on my lap, I think that allows you to call me either Gabriel or Gabe."

"And will you call me Mary?"

He nodded. "Forever, if I am so fortunate."

"I will not refuse," Mary whispered.

He reached down with his bandaged arm to retrieve something from between his leg and the chair. "I likely should not give this to you until we have married, but I am not always a patient man." He held out a small box. "Will you have me for your husband?"

Mary took the box and, opening it, gasped. Inside was a golden ring with a diamond surrounded by fifteen small rubies in the shape of a heart.

"You are my heart," Gabe said when she looked up from the beautiful ring to his face. "And I would give my very life to see you safe and happy."

Her lips quivered as happy tears gathered in her eyes. "You already have, or at least, you attempted to."

"I would do it again," he said as he stroked a finger along her cheek. "I need no warehouses, no business deals, no prize ships, or their bounty to be happy, Mary. I need only you, for you are my prize of greatest value. Please say you will be my wife."

Mary nodded and smiled as tears slid down her cheek. She placed the box and ring in her lap and cupped his face in her hands. "Yes. Yes, I will marry you, you dear, dear man. How could I not marry you when you hold my heart? I shall not love any other." She kissed him lightly.

"Kiss me again," he whispered, his dark desire-filled eyes held hers.

As she pressed her lips against his once again, he pulled her close, his bandaged hand cupping the back of her head. Slowly, he moved his lips over hers as if savoring every touch. Then, he pressed into the kiss more firmly, causing a swirl of lovely warm feelings to course through her, and as she sighed with pleasure, he delved deeper, tasting her teeth and flicking her tongue with his as his uninjured hand slid upward from where it held her at her waist until it rested just below her breast. With a groan, he broke the kiss and rested his forehead against hers. Her hands which had tangled themselves in his hair, returned to cup his face.

"I love you," she whispered.

"And I you," he replied. "And..." He pulled back and waited until she looked at him. "I shall never, ever let you take on water."

Such a statement could only be replied to in one way, and as desire once again built in them while they kissed and caressed one another, Mary knew that her heart had finally found a home where it would be protected. Always.

Before You Go

If you enjoyed this book, be sure to let others know by leaving a review.

~*~*~

Want to know when more books in this series will be available?
You can always know what's new with my books by subscribing to my mailing list.
(There will, of course, be a thank you gift for joining because I think my readers are awesome!)
Book News from Leenie Brown
(bit.ly/LeenieBBookNews)

~*~*~

Turn the page to read an excerpt of another one of Leenie's books

Tom: To Secure His Legacy Excerpt

[*Other Pens, Mansfield Park, Episode 4* begins where Mary's story ends and follows Tom Bertram as he attempts to become all that he should be while not losing his heart in the process.]

FROM CHAPTER 1

Morning crept its way across the room, first spilling over the windowsill and then creeping across the floor before slipping through the gap in the bed curtains.

Tom Bertram tossed an arm across his eyes to block its advance. He did not wish to wake just yet. There was a beautiful angel singing to him as she blotted his face with a cool cloth, and if he waited just a moment longer, he might be able to open his eyes in his dream and finally see her face.

He groaned. It was no use.

His angel had flown away once again, and he was left with only a memory of her voice.

He stretched and slowly rose to a sitting position. He needed to get dressed and start his day. He knew he needed to, but he had little desire to do so. Being responsible was far less enjoyable than being reckless.

He groaned again as he straightened his leg. Being reckless did come with its own set of complaints. His leg hurt less than it used to, but it was still a trial. Thankfully, according to the physician, the break had knit together as it should. However, the leg was still not as strong as Tom would like it to be, and it did ache rather a lot in the mornings after being motionless for so long as he slept.

He pushed his way out of his covers and, taking up the cane that stood next to his bed, he rose. Within half an hour's time, he would be able to rise without the use of the blasted thing, but first thing in the morning, he could not. It was as if his muscles protested rising more than his brain did.

After pulling the bell for his man, Tom began what he could of his ablutions while waiting.

"Your paper is waiting for you below," his valet said as he entered the room.

Reading the paper first thing in the morning, just like rising while it was still morning, was new for Tom. Being a respectable and responsible gentleman seemed to have many unsavoury costs. However, if he wished to recover even part of what he had lost of his and his brother's inheritance in his dissolute days, he must learn the part of a duty-bound gentleman. It was not his natural bent. It should be, but it was not.

He lifted his chin so that his man could complete his shaving.

It would likely be easier to face both the morning and his future prospects with greater equanimity if he had gone to bed at an earlier hour.

He chuckled to himself. Was that not what his father always scolded? *Tom, a baronet does not while away his hours in pleasure to the harm of his estate.* That was a lesson hard learned.

Tom dried his face and began the work of making himself presentably attired.

Before he began any study of his new gambling haunts today, he had a friend upon whom to call – a friend who was both fortunate to have survived the night and the reason for Tom's lack of rest.

It had been a late night, waiting to see if Gabe had recovered his boat. And then, there had been the time at Gabe's house while Tom had waited to hear the surgeon's evaluation of his friend's injuries.

Today promised to be one of great interest, for Gabe had promised to share the harrowing tale of his ordeal, and then...

Tom chuckled to himself as his man tied his cravat.

"Mr. Durward is planning to give up his bachelor state," Tom said to his man.

"My congratulations," his man replied.

"He is hoping to tie himself to Miss Crawford."

"Miss Crawford?" The man before him blinked. "The lady that was at Mansfield?"

Tom nodded. "The very one. Will not Edmund be shocked when I invite Mr. and Mrs. Durward for a visit someday?"

"Indeed!"

"She has changed," Tom added. "Fanny will be pleased to see the transformation. I am not certain how my brother will receive it. He is more reticent in things than his wife."

He gave himself a looking over in the mirror. He did cut a dashing figure even when he was being respectable.

"Have there been any letters from Mansfield?"

"No, sir, none yesterday and so far, none today. There were some invitations, which have been placed in your study."

Tom's least favourite room in his entire life had been the study. He still had to remind himself not to shudder at the word.

The study here in town was his, and his alone. His father had given him sole control of this town house after Tom had recovered from his illness ready to take on a new life – one that was not given over to pleasure. Therefore, this study, since it was his and his alone, did not have to be one of criticism and scolding. This study could be an agreeable and even friendly place.

He loved his father, but theirs was not a close relation-ship. He would not be as his father was. He would attempt to encourage his children to do well, of course, but not in the same way his father had. He would smile and praise his children from the beginning rather than waiting until one of them had been lost to her willful ways and another had nearly killed himself trying to be as unlike his father as was humanly possible.

"Would you see that some breakfast is sent to me in my study?"

"Of course, sir."

"And the paper," he called after his man.

He blew out a breath. It was time to begin in earnest his work of recouping his losses, although he had to admit that he was not entirely certain he understood all the workings of investing. Gabe would likely be able to help him find places to put his money that would earn him a healthy – but secure – return.

Gambling was not new to Tom. He had lost plenty of money at card tables, races, and the like. However, spec-ulating on shares and such was different. There was still the possibility of gain or loss, but the money he was using seemed to be somehow more valuable.

It was not, of course.

The money had not changed one wit. It was Tom who had changed. He saw things in such a different way now since his angel had saved his life those many long months ago. Perhaps if he were very fortunate, one day, he would get to see her face and thank her for her service. But for now, he would have to satisfy himself with his memories of her care and her songs.

Acknowledgements

There are many who have had a part in the creation of this story. Some have read and commented on it. Some have proofread for grammatical errors and plot holes. Others have not even read the story and a few, I know, will never read it. However, their encouragement and belief in my ability, as well as their patience when I became cranky or when supper was late or the groceries ran low, was invaluable.

And so, I would like to say *thank you* to Zoe, Rose, Betty, Kristine, Ben, and Kyle. I feel blessed through your help, support, and understanding.

I have not listed my dear husband in the above group because, to me, he deserves his own special thank you, for without his somewhat pushy insistence that I start sharing my writing, none of my writing goals and dreams would have been met.

~*~*~

For those who might be interested in some of the topics touched upon in this book (such as privateering), I have some of my research sources along with some visual inspiration pinned to a board on Pinterest. You can find that board at this link.

Other Leenie B Books

You can find all of Leenie's books at this link
bit.ly/LeenieBBooks
where you can explore the collections below
~*~
Other Pens, Mansfield Park
~*~
Touches of Austen Collection
~*~
Other Pens, Pride and Prejudice
~*~
Dash of Darcy and Companions Collection
~*~
Marrying Elizabeth Series
~*~
Willow Hall Romances
~*~
The Choices Series
~*~
Darcy Family Holidays
~*~

Other Novels ~ Novellas ~ Shorts

About the Author

Leenie Brown has always been a girl with an active imagination, which, while growing up, was both an asset, providing many hours of fun as she played out stories, and a liability, when her older sister and aunt would tell her frightening tales. At one time, they had her convinced Dracula lived in the trunk at the end of the bed she slept in when visiting her grandparents!

Although it has been years since she cowered in her bed in her grandparents' basement, she still has an imagination which occasionally runs away with her, and she feeds it now as she did then — by reading!

Her heroes, when growing up, were authors, and the worlds they painted with words were (and still are) her favourite playgrounds! Now, as an adult, she spends much of her time in the Regency world, playing with the characters from her favourite Jane Austen novels and those of her own creation.

When she is not traipsing down a trail in an attempt to keep up with her imagination, Leenie resides in the beautiful province of Nova Scotia with her two sons and her very own Mr. Brown (a wonderful mix of all the best of Darcy, Bingley, and Edmund with a healthy dose of the teasing Mr. Tilney and just a dash of the scolding Mr. Knightley).

Connect with Leenie

E-mail:
LeenieBrownAuthor@gmail.com
Facebook:
www.facebook.com/LeenieBrownAuthor
Blog:
leeniebrown.com
Patreon:
https://www.patreon.com/LeenieBrown
Subscribe to Leenie's Mailing List:
Book News from Leenie Brown
(http://eepurl.com/bS1el1)

www.ingramcontent.com/pod-product-compliance
Lightning Source LLC
Chambersburg PA
CBHW070927250626
47159CB00009B/3149